A VIOLATION
BY TED CAMPBELL

I dedicate this novel to my mother and my Grandma, Lizzie Mae - may she rest in peace. Thank you for teaching me how to pray and the power of faith.

Acknowledgment

Special thank you to the National Theatre Conservatory, class of 2000, SUNY Purchase Collage, the Westchester County School System, and New York's LGBTQ+ community for my solid education and passion for learning.

My incredibly supportive team of family, friends, and fellow artists nationwide

To God, for every day behind me and all that lies ahead…

TABLE OF CONTENTS

Ж

IN DENVER

Ж

I'd been in Denver only four months, and already I had scored a new boyfriend, allowance for a daily weed habit, and created significant confusion in an already crumbling marriage of seven years. My new lover – a small-time local hustler named Jamie – had access to whatever it was I wanted after a long day of rehearsal at the Denver Opera House. I was to play the leading role of Otello in Verdi's classic opera. I can't be sure with what – or when – Jamie started lacing our joints, but I didn't complain when I finally noticed the high was taking me even higher.

I craved some form of release at the end of the long days. The mounting pressure over the opening of our masterpiece was growing enormously. Anything that could take the edge off as the time moved closer to previews and eventually opening night was a welcome reprieve.

Otello would be my premier as the first black man in decades to play the role of The Moore in a primary production in a formal Opera house. Much was riding on my success. I could feel the expectation of every ear in that rehearsal room the moment I opened my mouth to deliver a single note. Most of the cast admired my mastery of the highly challenging role. But there were those amongst the listeners that couldn't wait to hear a slight crack in the melody or sway in the rhythm. Any hint that a black man was incapable of such operatic heights.

Each day I promptly went to rehearsal – a little hungover from the night of partying with Jamie – voice pitch-perfect and more ready to sing than my body and mind were willing to perform. The cast, crew, or director never mentioned the slouch in my walk or my grumpy attitude when I was offstage. When on stage, I became the tragically troubled hero. Sometimes during rehearsals, I felt possessed by the character. I played an unwavering support to my stage wife, Desdemona. She was also my real-life wife. My offstage life partner, Sara Grime.

Sara and I were not in love in the conventional sense. I am a Gay man. Though to the public, that's still just a rumor. I'm not out publicly. Sara was my brother's girlfriend while we grew up in Westchester County, New York, in the mountainous town of Peekskill. There, Sara and I began our studies in the classics under my mother, Anna Master, a music teacher at Peekskill High.

My father was also a professional musician. He played several instruments and made his living as an artist, recording and touring with many bands throughout our childhood. We lived in a modest three-bedroom house my parents could barely afford at the time on musician/teacher salaries. I remember being happy there. For a time, anyway.

Sara's father was also a teacher and musician at Peekskill High. He taught science. Sara's mother died when she was just a baby, leaving Mr. Grime to raise his daughter alone.

Mom met Mr. Grime as he stood in the doorway of her classroom one afternoon after school ended. He stood in the open doorway listening to her playing a jazz riff on the grand piano and scatting like Sarah Vaughan, as she would do when school let out for the day. Mama loved to sing. Mr. Grime told her that her voice drew him to the room. He told Mom he played the upright bass. She invited him to join a jam session at our house one weekend. During that first jam session at our house, I met Sara for the first time.

Even as a child, she was a beautifully enchanting girl. Her long, straight brown hair framed her thin face like a classic portrait of a young goddess. Her eyes were a silvery blue that captured one's gaze upon sight. She had naturally pursed lips that seemed organically painted cherry red. She'd always been a petite girl, regardless of age or how much she ate. Her power was in her presence, and it enriched as the years passed.

I remember that the tiny trio was in the garage one Saturday morning in the Spring –sometime in the nineties. Sara and I were in Junior High. Both were in the same grade and school but didn't know one another. I believe she transferred to our school that year. My father was at the drum set perched in the lot's corner, my mother on the upright piano they parked against the wall, and Mr. Grime had his cello in his arms, handling it like an old lover in the center of the garage space. The car park door was open, and Sara sat on a stool in its archway before the trio when I entered the space. She looked like a young agent from a music management firm in her loose blue jeans and white t-shirt decorated with butterflies across the chest. She was overly interested in the trio, I thought.

The tune was an improvised, upbeat number that accented Mr. Grime's skills on the bass. He played it like he'd been born with the instrument and practiced in the womb. Mom would holla a riff here and there without words, scatting above the instrumentation as if her voice were created solely to serve that purpose. Dad was the fantastic man on the drums. He sliced and sifted the rhythms like the leader of a grand orchestra. The entire improvisation sounded scripted and mature. Like they'd been playing together for many years.

Their music drew me to Sara's side. Her gaze at the wonder before her was more enticing than the act being played out. She didn't seem to listen to the tune but felt it. The trio played like we weren't even in the room with them. At one point, Sara closed her eyes and leaned her head back as my mother's riff soared through the scales with such ease that it sounded like what I'd guess was a hummingbird's soft melody.

"Your Mom was born with God's most amazing instrument." She said without opening her eyes. I didn't even know she knew I'd come up beside her.

"This is true," I said without hesitation. It was a well-known fact in our house.

"What's all this racket y'all got going on out here?" My brother Russell's voice brokered through the music. "A man can't even sleep in on a Saturday morning with all this noise coming out his garage. What are the neighbors going to say?"

"I'm thinking they'd offer a collection," Sara said. "The beautiful sounds coming out of here on such a lovely morning deserve just that." The trio broke the fourth wall to look at their captive audience and heckler. I remember the sun peeking out of the clouds like a smile rising on a sad face, leaking light into the dim garage.

"I'm sorry to disturb you, Russell," Ma said. "We were just trying to get Mr. Grime here to join our duet and form a trio to take on the road." She stepped away from the upright to pat Mr. Grime on the shoulder. He smiled back at her. Daddy just watched them. Then Ma looked back at Russel standing in the doorway in his mismatched pajamas and offered, "Maybe a little bacon and flapjacks will calm your nerves since we woke you up, old man." Ma guffawed at her seventeen-year-old son. Russel and I were four years apart. He is the older son.

"That would be nice," Russell said in his most sarcastic tone.

Sara shot a look of distaste toward him, but it was quickly diminished once she caught sight of his face. Their eyes locked, and at that moment, I knew our lives were about to change for the worse.

The bottom of Sara's red lips dropped slightly as she narrowed her eyes at my brother standing by the garage door leading into the kitchen. Russell was a strapping brown boy with a muscular build inherited from our father. Tall with a slim waist and thick, strong legs. But he had the soft features of our mother in the face. Her almond eyes, broad forehead, thick black lips, and nose perfectly fit the center of her face.

They blessed him with all the good stuff that makes a black man fine as hell.

I favored our father in the face. A big flat nose and broad mouth and ears that protrude out the sides of my head like a baby elephant. My head eventually grew into the ears.

Sara couldn't take her gaze off Russell the entire morning as we exited the garage and went into the kitchen for one of Mom's incredible breakfasts. We were just teens then.

The musical trio rehearsed every weekend in that garage through the end of junior high and all through my high school years. They performed all up and down the east coast. The group even recorded an album that earned my mom and dad enough money to pay off our little house in Peekskill.

Mama recognized the talent that Sara and I possessed. She began teaching us the singer's ways early in our teenage development. Through those lessons, Sara and I grew closer, fostering an unbreakable bond as musical siblings around the rise of our parent's Westchester trio.

I had inherited my mother's gift of song. And Mama was more than happy to encourage and help me nurture the gift. Sara's voice bloomed later, finally catching up with her natural musicality. We sang duets at parties and church functions all around the state of New York. When word got around about us, we were asked to travel south to sing for the people of Georgia, Alabama, and the Carolinas. Not just spiritual or gospel songs, but we had become known for mastering classical religious music by Bach and Brahms. Our classics intensified as our repertoire grew with our voices.

It was an incredible feeling to discover the power of my voice while studying the classics. Mama's training allowed me to stretch my voice beyond the limitations that secular and gospel music posed. I learned how to find freedom within the constraints of the carefully styled art songs of the early centuries. By age twenty, I was nearly a master of technique and had grown into a fine, strong tenor.

Sara also progressed, though not as strongly as I did. Her voice was still thin and shrill, in the higher range during her early twenties. She hid behind her natural musicality and struggled as Mama's student. They often fussed over Sara's lack of discipline. Sara would throw my mother's words back at her, reminding Mom that the female voice matured slower than the male instrument. Sara's thoughts also drifted further away from music and toward my brother, Russell.

My older brother was in his late twenties as Sara and I earned our master's degrees in vocal performance at SUNY Purchase College. He was a Westchester Community College drop-out, four times over, living at home, unable to hold down steady work. Ma and Daddy felt sorry enough for him not to put him out. Nothing stopped him from working out, looking good, and partying like a teenager. Despite all the affairs, Sara loved him through it. She would cry on my shoulder whenever Russell said something abusive or she found out about another woman he'd been with.

The two kept the courting a secret for as long as possible. Our parents were unaware of the two getting closer while the adults were away on gigs that sometimes took them out of town for days. Russell exposed their affairs to me when he asked me for money. I had my suspicions all along, though I kept them to myself. Sara was always sad whenever we'd hang together after classes. She didn't hide her curiosity about Russell's whereabouts or wonder who he was with when he wasn't home. And when he was around, the two of them would stow away in his bedroom with the door locked. And the nineties hip-hop music blared behind the door.

I questioned her about it. She laughed and called me jealous that I wasn't the center of attention. When Russell asked me for the money, he wouldn't initially disclose what it was for. After a great deal of prying and denying him the cash, he finally confessed to getting Sara pregnant. The two of them didn't want to keep the baby.

"You should tell Daddy," I said to him.

"Are you fuckin' crazy, boy? He'd string me up for sure." He told me. "You gonna loan us the money or not?"

I didn't do it until I talked to Sara. She was in tears when we talked after a movement class on campus. I drove us home to Peekskill. She was living with us by then. Her father stayed in the den when the trio was home.

"I don't want to do it," she cried. "But it would ruin any hope for a future. And my father would be furious with me. Please help us, Cameron. Please."

What was I to do? I made her promise that once this was done, she'd give up on Russell and get back into her studies. We'd find an agency together, move away from Peekskill to earn a living as working musicians and tour the world like our parents. For a time after the abortion, a music career was all we aimed for. It brought us even closer and pushed Sara further away from Russell. He started drinking heavily and kept late hours. Sometimes he wouldn't come home at all.

We found opera houses and agencies across the country and far away from home that was searching for singers. The salaries weren't much, but with second jobs and side gigs, I could see us making it work. I had even got a lead on an agency looking for a bi-racial couple to groom for the roles in Otello in productions to come around the world. Then tragedy struck a few blows before we could begin our future.

The Jazz album, recorded in the late nineties called 'Songbird' garnered the trio's attention on the west coast. They bagged gigs in Seattle, San Francisco, and Vegas and ended their west coast run in downtown Denver, Colorado, in an up-and-coming jazz club called the Blue Light Lounge. It was a weekend engagement.

The nineties ushered in a renewed interest in jazz music, with younger artists using instruments like the piano and guitar to express themselves in performance. The trio thought it best to ride that wave as long as it flowed. Once it went dry, they'd throw in the music sheets and chalk it all up to experience. My father handled all the management and the money.

It was during that weekend misfortune struck. Russell called our mother at the hotel they were staying in to tell Mom that Sara was pregnant. Yet again. He had tried to convince her to abort the child, but she refused. She couldn't go through with that again. The worst part was that Russell tried telling our mother the child wasn't his. He admitted to going with her. Even admitted to fathering the first child, but he lied to our mother, saying this child couldn't be his.

"She's been around since me, Ma," Russel told Mom. "It could even be Cameron's bastard, for all I know. They're always together these days, singing." I hadn't been with a woman then and never would in my future. Russell hung up on that call and later told me about it. He said Ma would talk to the fathers about the pregnancy, and they'd be home soon.

We did not hear from our parents for days after Russell's call. They didn't come home when they should have.

I saw a news story on television about a music trio visiting Colorado from New York. They had been victims of a murder-suicide in a hotel near the Blue Light Lounge. The incident happened the same night as their final performance at that same club.

It was a Saturday evening. I was making dinner. I called Sara into the kitchen. We watched in horror as the headshots of our parents flashed across the screen. I remembered Russell's call, and many thoughts circled as the reporter went into details about what the police suspected had happened at the hotel:

"The police are saying the drummer, band leader, and husband, Cameron Master, Sr., killed his band mates, Anna Master, also his wife, and Terry Grime, in a fit of rage while in a personal dispute over an incident unrelated to their gig at the Blue Light lounge. Neighboring guests at the hotel claimed to have heard Grime screaming about a daughter defiled by their derelict black boy. Another male voice cried out about an alleged affair. The neighboring patrons heard crashing and a woman's screams before the room went silent."

"The front desk was notified of the commotion; however, the police weren't called in until the band hadn't shown up for their final performance at the Blue Light

Lounge. The authorities had management open the door to the room occupied by the Master couple. There they found the horrific scene."

"Terry Grime, the trio's bassist, looked to be the first assaulted, trying to defend himself against an angry Master who stabbed his bandmate thirty times before turning on his wife, Anna Master, using the same blade. The room was in disarray. The officers then found Cameron Master, Sr., naked in the bathroom tub with the same knife against his throat, covered in blood. He claimed the devil forced his hand, and he was prepared to take ..."

"Turn it off!" Sara shouted. It took me a moment to register the words, but I did as she commanded. We both stood stone-still in the kitchen as if suspended in time. Neither of us could move from the shock of what we'd learned about the adults who'd raised us. I finally looked at Sara. I could see the shame emblazoned all over her pale face.

"How could he do something so..." she couldn't find the word.

But I could.

Savage, heartless, monstrous, heinous. I didn't say any of them. Though I had an idea of my father's reasons, I said nothing. We stood there in the kitchen, silent. I watched Sara raise a hand to her belly, which had yet to reveal the life growing inside it. She looked at me, terror-stricken.

We didn't see Russell again until he was found strung out in an alley on the Southside of the Bronx. Six months before, his daughter, Mya, was born into our lives. She was the spitting image of our mother, only with lighter skin. Sara took this as an omen. I could only see the curse that had brought a dark cloud over my life for years to come.

That's when I started – 'using.' It was the only solace I could find in the madness that grew around me. I married Sara out of pity and part guilt for things I could never have prevented. But I was angry with the world of music for taking my family away from me. Yet I strived in that same world. We both did.

Music brought us directly to where our parents were stolen from us many years ago. It was a city that held no significance until it snatched the lives of the musicians that loved and made us.

FIGHT NIGHT

Ж

I arrived in Colorado as a broken man. My lack of obligation and duty strained our marriage. Sara and I barely talked anymore. We had even traveled separately and stayed in separate quarters in the hotel during the rehearsal period. Mya was in the home my parents left me in Peekskill. She was with our Manny, Kyle. I knew he was sleeping with my wife. I didn't care. His relationship with my niece was more potent than the bond I shared with her, pretending to be her father. I'd become a lone note floating in the air of a quiet but empty cathedral. I could call it luck that I found Jamie when I did. Or I could take a more brutal look and see the trouble he posed from the beginning of our relationship. My supplier and my betrayer, I took what he offered willingly and never questioned where it might lead.

There were still a few nights before opening previews for Otello. Dress rehearsals tediously filled the days with stops and goes as the crew adjusted lights and set pieces positioned appropriately to appease the aesthetic our director, Danial Haywood, was going for. Danial never looked happy with the production. He conflicted with our conductor, Hazel Goings, about some musical entrances or exits of the thirty-six-piece orchestra. Where he beckoned precision, Hazel conducted loose and lofty. Her style was more familiar with the cadence written by the composer. She was more familiar with the piece than he and had no problem showing him that. They bickered constantly throughout the rehearsal process. In those final weeks of tech and dress, the bickering between them had elevated to full-on arguments that warranted clearing the theatre of the cast and non-essential crew members so that union time didn't go wasted on production disputes struggling to be worked out.

The cast got dismissed for the evening and promised an early morning call for a complete run-through of the show the next day.

I was thankful for it. Sara and I hadn't spoken since arriving in Denver. Our only form of discourse was on the stage and in song. We didn't share a hotel room. We never did on any gig. There was no sense in lying to ourselves about the true nature of our marriage. We were barely even friends since I began living out my sexual preference more openly than before. Mya was in school. I didn't think Sara would mind the affairs. It was no secret she and our Manny, Kyle, were seeing each other. Why was it a problem that I had taken on my own lovers? I stopped by her dressing room that evening, hoping for a word.

"Sara," I said as I knocked softly. There was no answer. "Can we talk?"

"Not tonight, Cam. I'm exhausted. I know we need words, but this role stretches me beyond my limits. Please..."

"You're beautiful in this role, Sara," I told her, giving all my affections to the closed door. "You sound like an angel during our duet. I forget I'm singing with you — I listen so intently to you." I wait for something from the other side. When there is nothing: "Please, Sara. Just a few minutes."

"I can't, Cameron." She said, her voice closer this time. "Not tonight. I need to rest my voice. Perhaps tomorrow. We'll have dinner. You should go back to your room and sleep tonight. Your attitude is never any good in the mornings. It's probably because you refuse to sleep. You can't always rely on your gifts, my darling." Those last words sounded more like a warning. She wouldn't tell me, but I knew what it was about. It was about Jamie, the drugs, and the parties. All the late nights since we arrived. And even before that. Back in New York. The late nights kept me from home and our pretend life. I want to tell her I'm suffocating.

"All right," I said. "If you can't..." I could hear a sigh of relief through the thick door. "Perhaps tomorrow then. Dinner?" I walked away from her dressing room door quickly. Already I could taste the drugs in my thoughts. I wanted to smoke — drink. I wanted to forget.

When I called Jamie from my hotel room, he was hardly the relief I'd hoped for. Before that day, he had never read an article in the local paper. He saw an article about the show and read it. He knew I was a married man. I disclosed that much to him when we started fooling around. But he did not know my wife was playing opposite me in the show. The local paper had disclosed that to him. He was furious with me. I tried to explain the situation, but he wouldn't listen. He wanted to drink, smoke pot, and whatever else he rolled in the joints we burned that night. He wanted to enjoy the Denver nightlife — as he put it—before we met up.

We scored some drugs in the park in front of the Capitol building from his good friend. He didn't have to pay. We were a few blocks away from his home at the Windbro Apartments. He stopped by his neighbor, Steven's, to ask if he wanted to join our private party. He hadn't said a single word to me during our entire quest. Not even a 'hello' or a welcoming kiss on the cheek when we met up. I tried to push the negative thoughts out of my head. I wanted to understand his jealousy toward Sara but couldn't wrap my head around it. Why did it matter that she was my wife in the eyes of the public? He was the one I shared a bed with, and she understood I did not love her in that way. We married for the sake of our daughter. My niece. Our Mya. Jamie wouldn't hear any of that. "She's your wife." I could hear his eyes say every time he glanced in my direction.

In the three months I'd secretly dated James 'Jamie' Peterson, I'd questioned his friendship with his neighbor, Steven Abrey. Both white men in their mid-thirties died blonds, both slenderly built with catered upper bodies and flat but tight tiny asses. They could easily be brothers, but their effeminate behavior gave them away as something slightly more than friends. Jamie was naturally masculine whenever he and I were together alone. Never a high pitch in the tone of his voice or a sway of the hip when he walked. Steven brought those traits out in him whenever he was around. Steven's natural walk swayed and had 'sex like a stripper' in it as he sauntered around. A female stripper. Every movement he made seemed to beg for male attention, and he knew men watched him, even when the stares were unfavorable. Steven enjoyed touching and fondling my man in familiar ways I thought were unacceptable. Jamie would say it was harmless when I confronted him about it.

Sometimes they'd banter like an old married couple. They kept secrets from me, knowing I was watching them—giggling and smiling in my direction. Teasing my intuitions. The entire dirty business seemed clear to me that night after rehearsal.

The three of us spent the late-night Gay bar hopping after smoking-up in Jamie's apartment. We crawled into a yellow cab at the Compound bar to head back to Jamie's place to get even higher.

I woke suddenly from my wide-eyed inebriated haze as I spotted the church across the street from the Windbro Apartments. I thrust my open palm at the dashboard and jolted forward, alerting the driver to stop. The dark-skinned black driver of our vintage yellow cab slammed the brakes to bring the car to a sudden stop, jerking us all forward.

Jamie and Steven giggled in the backseat.

"Here?" The driver asked in what sounded like a West African dialect.

I wiped the light sweat from my brow. "Yeah," I said.

Jamie and Steven were drunk, talking, singing, and fooling around like they were the ones in love. Jamie was trying to make me jealous. I feared, all night, that Steven saw our scuffle as his opportunity to pull Jamie away from me and into his arms. And from all the ruckus in the backseat, he was getting exactly what he wanted.

I paid the driver with whatever bill I pulled out of my wallet. It must have been enough. The golden smile of crooked teeth in his round, jet-black face widened into a grin. He nodded incessantly until I got out of the passenger's side door. I didn't mean to slam the car door. My blood was boiling. I didn't bother to look back. Jamie and Steven were probably still horsing around in the backseat. A sudden pang sent a sharp pain shooting through my core. It was quick, like glasses falling from a counter and breaking to pieces on the floor. The shattered sickles pricked away at my insides.

I walked to the entrance of the Windbro, then finally looked back. I saw the two of them stumbling out of the backseat door of the yellow cab, lustfully laughing in open-mouth kisses and groping one another like they were about to fuck like wild dogs. Right there in the street next to the yellow cab. The African driver stared down at them, wide-eyed, then looked up at me—smiling and shrugging his shoulders.

At that moment, everything in my sight turned blood red.

The sign in front of Jamie's building, the church across the street, the yellow cab, the brown face of the driver—all of it saturated in a red rage that fueled my next step.

The pricking rage inside of me forced my body forward, running. My arms outstretched, my fingers in a clutch at the ends of my palms; my body hurling toward Jamie, freshly released from a passionate embrace with his neighbor and long-time friend.

I pushed Steven to the ground. Hard. My hands locked around Jamie's throat, tight as a vice grip. The force of the impact took us down to the pavement. When his head hit the ground, I did not stop. Vigorously, I attacked his face with closed fists. Any care I felt for him had turned in on itself and brought out a monster I didn't know was a part of me—a part of our love.

I couldn't get control of myself. I didn't want control. I fed into the raged possession. A swelling heat burned my eyes, soaking my brown face with hot sweat. The rage controlled every strike until Jamie's face was a bloody, matted mess. He lifted his head off the ground and, with a quick reflex, forced my fist into the middle of his chin. I struck him so hard that the back of his head smacked the pavement. I heard a loud crack in the quiet night streets. Jamie's eyes spun to the whites. There was a shrilled, girly scream that swirled above me. It wasn't a woman's shout. It was a man squawking like a girl he hoped to be but never would.

I looked up to find Steven huddled in the darkness of the Windbro's night shadow. He sported his bright pink mini shirt wrapped around his boney body like bubble gum on a child's tiny finger. His white, pencil-legged denim jeans and silly platform sneakers made him look like a flamingo lost in a concrete jungle.

"Stop!" He shrilled. "You're going to kill him."

Jamie spat between my legs, a laugh mixed with blood and a hard cough. His eyes were back from the whites. He looked lucid enough to say plainly: "I guess somebody's going to miss opening night." A bloody burst of coughing laughter convulsed from him then.

That rage—I felt its power seize me. I'd been humiliated by Jamie long enough, betrayed! My weighty fists beat down on his head once again with no mercy. I watched his face morph in and out of bloody shapes.

"Please! Stop this." Steven's womanish scream pleaded. "We were teasing you. We were fucking with your head. You're going to kill him! Stop it, Cameron!"

Wide-legged, I stood over Jamie's indolent body, staring deep into the red darkness where the man flamingo quivered. I felt like a rabid dog looking to sink his teeth into something. It felt nothing like me. It wasn't me. Yet I understood this rage like it had been my old friend paying a visit. I could smell the sweet sweat of Steven's girly spray mixed with a soured, manly odor. It infuriates me even more. All of this was wrong.

The street was so quiet I could hear our hearts beating. Mine is from adrenaline. I think his heart beat faster from fear. Jamie's heartbeat was faint. Nearly not even there. I believe I heard Steven pray in the still blackness. Rationality was long gone, though. My soul was released into the rage of possession. It knew me. I had no reason to fight it anymore.

"I'm so sorry." Steven whimpered.

Red, white, and blue lights flashed behind me before I could step toward him. Two police cars jumped the curb, blocking our grungy scene on all sides. The sirens whaled when the cars stopped. I slightly turned to face the men when a robust baritone voice warned me not to move. They were out of their cars with palms at the butt of their guns. Eager to fire if I disobeyed a command.

"Get your hands in the air!" Another voice screamed. This one was tinier, squeaky like a rusted wheel, but firm. "Now!" I did as he ordered.

My hands raised high above my head; I felt an overwhelming energy pass through my body like a flood of smoke escaping a burning house, like waking from a nightmare. My eyes darted around the scene, checking for something I knew was there but could not see. The crimson haze over the world faded. I couldn't be sure of what I had done. Had it happened at all?

I looked between my wide-legged stance. I saw Jamie's body lying still beneath me. His face was a mass of blood and abrasions. Both eyes were swelling. An egg-shaped lump over his left eye formed.

Had I done all this?

"Step to the left of the body!" The baritone shouted. I did as he said, watching at least for Jamie's still body to take in a breath. *Please, God.* A strange and sinister laugh erupted inside my mind. I knew it wasn't anything from my imagination. I knew it wasn't me inside my head. I panicked.

"Jamie." I leaned into the body, and four powerful hands grabbed my arms and swiftly took me to the sidewalk, face first. My head hit the pavement so hard I thought I would pass out. It sobered me steadfastly.

"He told you not to move, boy." The squeaky voice said. "Officer Downs, you get this black bear in the police car. I'll see what the other guy has got to say about all this." The cop pointed a flashlight beam into Jamie's face. He lay beside me, still motionless. "This one's not going anywhere till the medics get here." The officer said.

Officer Downs cuffed me tight and yanked me to my feet by the chain between the shackles. My chest heaved an incredible breath of mountain air into my lungs. That one breath—I'll never forget that one extraordinary, crisp breath of free fresh Denver night air.

That's when I remember hearing the whispering.

Thinking back on it now, I'm sure the voices were with me the whole night. Probably since I set foot on Colorado grounds. The drugs, the alcohol, the music, and the laughter of the club crowd drowned them out. In the quiet of the tainted red night, I could hear them clearer, creeping up the sidewalk and hiding behind bushes lining the street. They raced through a language I didn't understand, running a prayer or a chant in a foreign, menacing tongue that flickered like a rattler's tail. I tried to nudge them away with my shoulder. They kept coming for me.

Officer Downs tightened his grip on my right arm. He turned me toward the blinding lights of the police car. I flicked my head over my left shoulder to check on Jamie again.

The other cop, a white officer with a buzz cut, close-cropped hair, and a stout, stocky build, flashed his beam down on Jamie again, only quicker this time. He walked away before I could get a second look at Jamie's face.

"You're not going to check his pulse?" I shout at him. I was almost turned back into the scene when Downs tugged hard at my arm.

"Listen, my brother…" he said. The menacing whispers grew louder in my head.

The white officer turned around so quickly that I thought he would draw his gun and shoot. "Officer Downs? Would you get that man in the car? There's been enough trouble in the quiet for one night. Am I clear?" Though he talked to Downs, his gaze was fixed on me before he haughtily turned back to Steven, standing like a statue in the doorway of the Windbro. The horrified look on Steven's face made it seem as if I'd assaulted him. The cops didn't give me the chance to.

"My brother," Downs said quietly, "you don't want to make this harder for yourself."

"I ain't your brother, you black pig." I heard the words come out of my mouth, but I swear they were not my intent. The Whispers told me what to say. They spoke for me. I quelled my anger before I acted on the urge to spit in Downs' face. He yanked me forward. Walked me to the back of his police car. He pulled the door open with a thrash and huffed to tuck me inside the cavernous backseat.

"Watch your head." He mumbled graciously as I dipped inside.

Downs had a broad center. He was tall and looked like he had once been a bodybuilder or had just started working out and was getting a more toned upper body. He was brown-skinned with plain features on his face. A short-cropped afro topped his milk-dud round head. I'm sure his look would have been genuinely kind if he wasn't so angry with me. There was no reason for me to mistrust him, but the Whispers in my head would not allow me to soften enough to apologize to him. Looking at him through the backseat window as he watched his partner talking to Steven, my lips curled into a tight, anger-filled ball. I couldn't understand how I was moving these muscles against my will. I shook my head. The Whispers quieted. They seemed to dance around in the carriage. Bouncing off the windows and shaking the gate that separates me from the driver's console in the front seat. I tried to push the tip of my right shoulder into my ear to escape the insisting sound. It was telling me to do something. Nagging at me to act. I couldn't understand the words. The intent was clear. Whatever this buzzing was, it didn't like authority and wanted me to do something about it. The back seat suddenly felt blazing hot, like a one-hundred-degree summer. And rising.

Downs hopped into the front seat. He stared through the windshield at his partner and Steven, who flailed his arms while he parroted the night's events to the bored-looking officer taking notes. What about my side of the story?

The whispering intensified.

When I saw the ambulance turn onto the block, I heard the siren wail momentarily. The EMTs jumped out of the back and side of the wagon to prepare Jamie for the gurney. Steven stopped flailing to watch them. He covered his mouth and clutched himself as he watched. This gesture maddened the whispering in my head, sending them into an uproar. I wanted to curl up in the back seat like a frightened child in a bad storm.

"You alright back there?" Downs asked. "Still coming down from that fight, huh?"

And perhaps other things as well. I'd be a fool to mention the voices spinning webs in my ears. I didn't respond at all. Afraid of what I might say. I fixed my eyes on Jamie, hoping for any sign that he was alive.

Take a breath, damn you!

The Whispers hissed back at my thoughts. They sounded like sinister laughter.

"I know who you are?" Downs said suddenly. Everything seemed to stop momentarily—even the whispering. I pretended not to hear him. Hoping against hope, he didn't utter the words I heard.

"You're that singer in the show at the Opera House downtown." Downs went on. "Am I right?"

It surprised me that a black man of the law had heard of me or even thought to recognize me. Despite my skin color, I wasn't nearly as popular a singer as most in the industry. I'd received the role of Otello primarily because I was black—a dark black. Our director protested I was too young to sing the challenging role. Yet, I was the only black man called to audition. The producers insisted. The Denver Opera House wanted to be the first to abolish blackface in producing the classic. It became their mission to lead the charge toward diversity in the industry. And I was to be their herald.

"I wouldn't pin you as an opera lover," I said. I wryly smiled in what felt like a small, confused way. Downs was watching me through the rearview mirror. The EMTs were loading Jamie's body into the ambulance now. The Whispers simmered again like a resting pot of water.

"I'm not." Downs said. "My fiancé is a big fan of the stuff. She studied in college. She's an amazing singer. She's been following you and your wife since last year. Now–your wife! That woman can sing. She's got a voice like a lark…"

"Don't talk about my wife."

The cabin abruptly went silent.

"What's the deal with you, brother?"

I didn't bother to open my mouth again. Afraid of what might fly out of it against my will. They had loaded Jamie into the wagon. The workers, the officer, and Steven stood around the back of the open double doors as if negotiating what to do next. Then Steven climbed into the back of the ambulance and sat beside the gurney. He rubbed Jamie's arm. He turned his gaze outward. I swear he could see me through the cop car windshield and the backseat cage. His scowl read 'savage' all over.

The whispering kicked up in my ear again. The words like demands that would wreak significant penalties if not met. I realized then that the voices weren't talking to me. The orders weren't instructions for me to follow. One hissing was leading to the other. It seemed they noticed I'd discovered this, and they didn't like it.

"You want to tell me how all this got started, brother?" Downs said. "It might do you some good to get it out…"

"I told you I ain't your fuckin brother, you black pig!" I heard myself say. "My mammy wouldn't give birth to no black swine like you." I had no idea where those words came from, even after I'd said them. The cabin went silent again. But the whispering didn't stop. I could feel them wrestling inside my head as if wearing for my soul or fighting to own it. I saw Downs staring at me through the rearview mirror with more disgust in his eyes than Steven had thrown from the back to the ambulance.

"What are they talking about? My friend could die in that damn wagon…"

"And you might have killed him." Downs finished as he stirred in the front seat. He opened the car door and got out, then leaned his head in to look back at me. "I'm thinking you'll need a little time alone to stew on that one." He exited the car and leaned in to add, "Man." He slammed the car door behind him. I was too ashamed to tell him the voices in my head made me talk like that.

They wasted no time creating an irritating buzzing sound that hissed at both my ears like horseflies. I felt like I was in the middle of a fight, and the winner would eat away at my thoughts until there were none. Manically, I shook my torso, trying to beat off the growing chant as the voices joined forces to get control of my head. Then there was a voice that spoke words I could finally understand. It said, "I ain't done with you yet, boy."

The voice came from the seat beside me.

I tried not to turn my head to the right of me. I was deathly afraid of what I'd find there. There was no one else in the car when Downs loaded me inside. But something profound, mocking, sour in tone and texture spoke to me clear as the surrounding night. A southern drawl in that voice felt like a time much earlier in American history. An unpleasant time. A time only imagined in my nastiest nightmares.

A rotting sent like a million dead men ferment the backseat cabin. The putrid odor was so foul I dry heaved to keep the taste out of my throat. I could feel a presence in the seat next to me. I had to look.

Slowly, I turned my head, and what I saw there frightened me into silence. Sitting beside me was something like a living shadow of a man, not all there. From the moon and the streetlights glaring through the police car window, the bottom portion of a deadly pale face is shown. The sharp narrow chin was square and housed a thin mouth that barely had lips. Between them dangled a cigarette. Out of the shadowed center of the man rose a lit match. The tiny flame met the end of the cigarette. When the flame touched the cigarette, it acted as a wick to a firecracker, eating away at the smoke until it reached the thin mouth. The half-body ruptured into flames.

The Whispers made a final and loud attempt at my ears. The entire backseat of the police car burst into a blaze, and I was inside it with something I knew could not be human. Me and whatever he was were in the center of those flames as if cremating together. It would char me in seconds if I didn't get out of there.

But then I realized I couldn't feel the heat of the flames blazing away in the air. I felt nothing. The fire didn't move like a natural fire would. The flames danced softly as they flickered, then dispersed into black mist. The fire moved slowly, swirling through the gate between the back and the front cabin. The Shadow Man had vanished into a flame. Those flames danced through the gate links.

While the backseat burned, I looked into the open back of the ambulance and caught Steven's dreadful scowl again, more ferocious and madder than before. Jamie sat up on the gurney like a zombie rising to grace and joined Steven's haunting stare. His face seemed more beaten than when they pulled me off him. The egg-shaped knot above his eye had grown, distorting his head to make him look alien. He raised an eyebrow, half smiled, then waved at me slowly. The look on his face was hollow, emotionless.

What the hell had he put in those joints we smoked? I wondered.

Officer Downs, his partner, and the EMT workers talk amongst themselves as if nothing were happening around them. Then I heard the curling cackle of the Shadow Man's laughter before the fire vanished from the backseat.

I heard a door slam shut. Before they could close the second door to the ambulance, I caught a last look at Jamie, motionless, laid out on the gurney again. Steven stared down at him, stroking his arm and talking to him. The second ambulance door slammed. The EMTs got into the wagon and sped off into the night. The sirens blared, and the lights flickered, signaling their journey's urgency.

"Jamie!" I cried out. The sirens drowned out my cry. I began kicking and beating the seats so hard that the cruiser started rocking like a cradle. When Officer Downs opened the car door to get inside, I felt all the heat rush out into the open air as if escaping danger. Downs mentioned nothing about my screaming tantrum. It was like it didn't happen. He had not seen the burning Shadow Man or the backseat on fire. He took one last somber look at me through the gate before starting the squad car and driving off.

His partner followed in the second car, not far behind us. No sirens of flashing lights cut into the silent darkness as we cruised through the downtown Denver streets. I was completely frightened into silence.

What in the hell had Jamie given me? I repeatedly warned him to stop putting extra in the joints, being so close to opening night. Oh God! The show. The last four months of rehearsal flashed back to me like a vision of life gone by before a tragic death. I would have to get word to the theatre. The company would never forgive me for this. They need me.

"Is my friend going to be all right?" I finally asked Downs. "Did either of you ask the paramedics…"

"What's with you, man? If we hadn't restrained you when we did, you would have killed that so-called friend of yours." He stared into my eyes through the rearview mirror and the gate between us as we waited at the red light. His graying beard of thick facial hair and sincere brown eyes shamed me. I did not know this man but felt I'd disgraced him terribly. I suddenly thought about all the people I'd let down because I couldn't control my temper or habit.

"What are you high on?" Downs asked. "I know you're high on something?"

"I don't want to talk about it with you. Do you hear me?" I said sharply as the light turned green and the cruiser moved forward again. I wanted to spill my guts to Officer Downs. Unload my woes about Jamie, Steven, and my wife, Sara. Talk to him about my daughter/niece, Mya. Tell him everything that had gone wrong in my life that brought me to this moment. Tell him that the role I was to play at the Denver Opera House would jumpstart my dying career in classical music. Beg for his sympathy to set me free to right this wrong alone.

I heard the cackling laughter of the Shadow Man echo in my head.

The high from the drugs picked up as the adrenaline rush slowed my heart, and the race car rushed blood coursed through my veins. The world slowed as the police car whisked passed closed coffee shops, ladies' boutiques, nightclubs, and sleeping highrises against the crisp night sky. It was too dark to see the Rocky Mountains in the view. We were probably too low in the city to catch a glimpse. I looked for them anyway. I was trying to find peace in all the chaos I'd caused. I beat my lover to a pulp on the sidewalk in front of his home. I didn't even know I had that kind of anger in me. Where had it come from? I didn't know what to think about the hallucinations or the Shadow Man. I was high. That feeling while I beat Jamie, though... It was like someone had moved my soul aside and started to drive my limbs for me.

The Master family tragedy came back to me in such a rush I thought I would relive the trauma of that day all over again in the backseat. Sara and I listened to the reporter give the police officer's account of what the rage in my father had done to ruin our lives forever; that horrifying night in this same city so many years ago.

Had that rage found me? I remembered my brother's shame at our father's hostile actions. It was a shame that drove him closer to drug abuse, madness, and eventual suicide. I thought I was above all that back then. Look at me now. Strangely, I was a victim of that same shame. Only I was the fool to believe I had overcome.

I closed my eyes to forget and saw Jamie and Steven in a more profound kiss than the one they shared in front of the Windbro apartments. My blood boiled all over again. But there was no one to fight in that backseat but me. Me and all my demons.

I'd been warned about my temper in the past. Before I found an agent and started making a name for myself in the industry, I sang in a church choir on the Upper Eastside of Manhattan. It was a well-to-do organization with extremely wealthy parishioners attending service religiously. They loved well-done quality music at Sunday service and weren't modest when paying for it. The choir met every Wednesday, Friday, and Saturday to rehearse for service on Sunday. The choir director, Arty Jennings, was a real bastard, but he knew his classical music. We didn't get along. He told me once that he never thought classical music was designed to fit my people. "No offense," he told me once at a holiday party, "I could never get used to seeing a black woman playing Mimi. Even Otello is done in blackface. Why would they ever hire you to sing the role?" The pay was good, so I tolerated his heavy-handed ignorance and attended as few church functions as possible.

One Wednesday night, while rehearsing a featured piece with the choir, surprisingly, I wasn't in a good voice, and Jennings decided to embarrass me in front of the entire group. He stopped our pianist with a grand wave of his thin white hand just as I entered the second verse of my solo and whaled about my diction. He said, "This isn't some crooner song produced by Motown songwriters. This is Brahms!" I could almost hear the 'N-word' at the end of his sentence; he spoke the words with such hatred.

I didn't speak. I just reacted.

Jennings was within arm's length of my right hand. I reached out and grabbed his neck. Before I could stop myself, I smacked him in the head several times. It was Sara's hand on my hot cheek that stopped my anger. She said, "Don't let his ignorance get the better of you." I let Arty go immediately as if waking from a sick dream. I walked away from that choir job that night. When Sara arrived home, she told me the church would not do without me and wanted me back. They would find another director. Everyone in the church, even our accompanist, vouched for me to the church board the next meeting day. I was forgiven, but it was made clear to me that violence, under any circumstance, would not be tolerated. I promised it would never happen again. Arty Jennings was not let go, but we never had words of any kind again. I stayed with the choir another year and found my agent Fay Warner. My career took a turn for the better then.

ARREST

Ж

Our squad cruiser pulled into a parking lot in front of a large grey building with thin windows. It was tall and wide and stood alone behind the Capitol building at the far end of the city park. It looked like a menacing old castle out of a fantasy novel. They designed the peaks of the building like points at the top of an evil king's crown. Against the dark sky, the grey mass almost vanished. If it wasn't for some lights shining through the slender windows on different floors, the towering structure would go unnoticed. I would never have guessed it was the Denver county holding jail. It looked more like a scary museum or a haunted castle removed from an amusement park to threaten Denver's wicked.

Jamie had scored drugs in the park several afternoons before, and I'd seen the building in the distance while waiting for him. It's hard to miss during the day. When I'd asked him about it, he shrugged his shoulders with a 'what do you care?' look. He did not know what it was, either, I bet. It's strange to me how fate has a way of making things clear.

Downs pulled into a reserved space in the parking lot filled with other police cars. He got out without another word to me. He didn't even look back to ensure I hadn't found a way out. He greeted a colleague in the lot, and they talked near the car's trunk. I remember thinking: my arrest must be the night's highlight if they've got time to waste on chit-chatter. I wanted out of these cuffs and on the phone. There was no way I was going to be held there overnight. It was a Thursday night. Jamie told me once that if you didn't see a judge on a Friday morning when you got locked up, you'd be in holding the entire weekend. Otello went into previews that weekend.

That putrid stench fermented the backseat again. It rose quickly, filling the cabin with the sour smell of rotting meat burned to the bone. I was getting hot. I wanted to take off my shirt; it was so hot. Then there was that cackling laughter, staccato and barely audible. I couldn't tell if it was in my head or the seat next to me.

I began to kick and rock. I shoved around the car's interior until it bounced so hard that a chit-chatting Officer Downs nearly fell. I writhed and railed in that backseat, afraid to encounter what I had seen earlier. Unwilling to revisit the horror. I needed fresh air.

When the door burst open, the heat and scent escaped faster than it came. I rolled out of the car. My feet hit the ground hard before my upper body flopped forward like a rag doll. I looked down at a shiny pair of black boots as I vomited all over them. The laughter, like blaring music from a passing car, whizzed past my ears and into the night.

"Wilson, no!" When I looked up from the mess I had made of those shiny black boots, I found Downs holding back the strike of a white officer with a billy club raised high above my head. "They're just boots, officer." Downs said. "Just boots."

"I should make him lick 'em clean."

"I bet you'd enjoy that," I said through a cough. With my meanest stare, it felt like I dared Wilson to hit me. I hadn't felt that brave since I was a wild kid in grade school.

Downs got the billy club out of Wilson's hands before I felt a hard slap against my right cheek. It forced my head to knock on the door frame. "I could take this one inside for you, Downs. If you want to get back on the road."

"I bet you would, Deputy Wilson." Downs said, pulling me out of the seat and slamming the back door. "I got it from here. You better go clean off your boots."

The deputy had sloshed some of the mush from my stomach onto my shoes and the bottoms of my pant legs. A strong smell of whisky and stomach juices wafted up into my nose from the ground. My head ached. The pain bounced around my skull like toddlers learning to tap dance.

Downs tugged at my arm, causing the cuffs to cut at my wrists. I wanted to cry out, but I didn't. Some new part of me wanted this abuse.

Deputy Wilson waddled from us, shaking his feet to get the lingering muck off his boots. He was cursing something awful. I couldn't help but smile at his foolish behavior. Downs shoved me toward the gray sandstone building entrance. As we got closer to it, I couldn't take my eyes off the menacing structure. The few lights shining through the thin slithering horizontal windows seemed to make out a face like an enormous jack-o'-lantern against the starless city sky. Then an entire row of horizontal lights burst high and flickered like a lightning bolt struck the building. There was not a cloud in the sky. It frightened me still. Forcing Officer Downs to run into me from behind.

"Listen, boy. I don't have time for your antics tonight. You need to move on." He said.

"Did you see that?"

"You're high." He shouted. Annoyed. He walked around to face me. "You stop short once more, and I will knock your ass out myself. I'll drag you into the station and cuff you to a metal bench for the night. You want that?"

I didn't answer. I didn't like the way he yelled in my face. It made me feel like I was a child. No one spoke to me that way anymore. He stepped toward me, really getting in close. His breath was hot and sour.

"I asked you a question, choir boy." His voice had changed along with his demeanor. He sounded like someone I knew but had only just met and couldn't remember the voice. He sounded terrifying. It forced the response out of me.

"I don't want that, sir," I said, lowering my face to look at my messy shoes.

"Good. Let's go." He stepped behind me again and gave me a nudge forward toward the entrance door.

Inside the station, he cuffed me to a chair as promised. It was made of hard tan wood and had a leather cushion sown into the seat. It wasn't a plush armchair or a lazy boy in a fancy hotel lobby, but it was a far cry from the metal seat

Downs warned me about. I was grateful. Downs had me fill out a medium-sized white card with Miranda Rights on the back and a signature line at the bottom. I signed it. Then he flipped the card over and pulled an ink pad out of a drawer in his desk. He took my fingerprints. While he worked, he tried to get information out of me, pretending to be an old friend I should confide in. Through the haze of my high, I could see beyond his roost. He was an officer of the law. From his perspective, I was a suspect at the scene of a crime he was called to answer. He needed me to say something to incriminate myself. I didn't speak a word. I worried, though. Worried this was more serious than I'd bargained for. Perhaps they had detained me because Jamie was seriously injured. They'd have to make sure I didn't get away.

I looked down at my hands with their blackened fingertips. I turned them over to the backsides and found open scars and scratches from the fight. My knuckles were bruised and blackened. An aching began where the wounds were. All I wanted was to return to my hotel room, soak them in ice, take a hot shower, and fall into my plush bed. I wanted to forget this night. I wanted another joint. I'd settle for a stiff drink.

"I need to make a call," I told Downs as he put away his booking equipment. It was a barren workspace, like all the others in the large but cramped room. Some desks, chairs, filing cabinets, or officers took up every inch of the space. It must have been a rowdy night because they packed the room with men cuffed to chairs. Officers filing paperwork or getting prints. I suddenly heard the chatter of a debate between criminal and cop fill the space in the room's air. An officer was working his way out of another door with a belligerent, cuffed accused while two other officers grabbed their jackets and ran out another door in what looked like a hot emergency. Someone else had probably let his life spin out of control that night. A vagrant hollered protest. Another door slammed, and I nearly jumped out of my skin. I must have looked like the giant goose in the entire coop to the other hardened criminals. I looked around to be sure no one was watching me. I couldn't believe my part in this circus.

To the right and slightly behind me, I saw a white cop and a young white boy dressed in a t-shirt talking excitedly to the officer. His gestures were erratic, and the expressions on his stark, chiseled face filled with mirth. Suddenly, he stopped talking, calmly looked over his left shoulder, and stared directly at me. His hair was a firing red buzz cut. He wore a goatee of that same color around his thin mouth. His skin was as pale as the moonlight. The officer, too, looked up from his notepad, but his face had no features under the cap. Something like a swirl morphed in the middle where his nose should be. Then the entire room went utterly still— quiet as a theatre before the curtain rose and the show was about to start. Slowly, everyone in the room turned their gaze to me. I could feel the stares of even the people behind me. Not a word was spoken. The phones didn't ring. There was no sound from a typewriter—pure icy silence. The strangest part was that all the eyes felt like they were coming from one pair.

I turned back to look at Officer Downs, and he was turned away from me, reaching for the office phone on his desk. Everything went back to normal then. I looked back for the redhead boy and the officer, and they were gone. Vanished. I remember something different about the officer. His uniform was like an earlier model than Downs', like he was from the same police force just at an earlier time in history. The boy, too, looked like he didn't belong in the now either. I tried to find them as I looked around the room. Downs placed the phone in front of me on the desk.

"Looking for someone, choir boy?" He said.

"I'm no choirboy," I said. Very annoyed with myself and this whole scene. "I need to make a call. Get someone down here to bail me out of this shithole…"

"I know you don't think you're leaving here tonight." Downs said with a grin on his face. "Maybe not until Monday. If you're lucky."

"I can't stay in here till Monday. I've got a show to sing. You said you knew who I was…"

"I do." Downs said, still grinning. I was glad one of us was amused. "That doesn't change the crime scene we found you in the middle of on that street corner." His voice was stern, restrictive. I felt my shoulders sink.

He picked up the receiver and put it between my shoulder and ear. I held it there with my uncuffed hand so it wouldn't fall. He asked me for the number to call. The only number I could think of was the hotel room of my wife. She would be asleep at this hour. Not at all concerned with where I was or what I was doing. He dialed the number I gave him.

We were married in the first trimester of her pregnancy. It was the only time we had to conceal the baby and make it seem that I was the father. Faye Nelson, our manager, had taken us both on as her clients just after the wedding. She was familiar with our history and thought as we did about Sara's career. An unwed, single mother would have a more challenging time getting work in the churches that would pay top dollar for professional singers. But the two of us together would allure clients from all over the globe. When Mya came along, we were getting a name for ourselves in the industry, and our lie got better established. The pregnancy brought us even closer in those months. We were always on gigs singing art songs all around the U.S. in high demand. We shared hotel rooms in each city we visited for a while to keep up our deception. Eventually, it became irrelevant to do so. The bond we had to work so hard to build faded once my brother committed suicide. In a small way, I resented Sara in my silence. She and Russell's carelessness killed my family and tore her and me apart. I couldn't let her know how I truly felt. Instead, I stayed out nights and came in piss-poor drunk early mornings. I'd sleep all day to avoid them and hurry off to rehearsal or whatever show we were working on before they could catch me. There were so many affairs I had stopped counting. I'm sure she did, too. Mya hardly knows me. Or her real father. Or the family killed her grandfather.

The phone rang twice before I heard Sara pick up the line with a question in her clear voice, as lovely as a violin, even when awakened out of sleep in the middle of the night. "Hello? Who is this?"

"Sara, it's me. Cameron." I said. There was a long pause before I could find the words to go on. "I need you to call the company—call Danial and let him know that I've been arrested, and they need to bail me out."

"Arrested!" She was awake now. "What did you do to get yourself arrested?"

"I had a fight."

"You've been drinking. You've been doing drugs."

"I had a little of both. That has nothing to do with this…"

"It has everything to do with this, Cameron Grime!" She said. "What exactly do you expect me to tell Danial when I wake him up at night? His leading man is in jail days before we open because he got in a drunken street fight? With who, Cameron? Who were you fighting?"

"You know who…"

"No! I don't know. I want you to say it." Her voice was calm as a cold breeze.

"Are you going to help me or not?"

She was quiet for a long moment. I thought she had hung up on me. "I will see you in the morning." The line went dead.

Downs took the receiver from my ear, hung up the line, and put the phone back on the far end of the desk. I felt alone in Siberia without a coat or winter clothes.

"Get up." Downs ordered after he released the cuff from the chair.

I was so shocked that I could hear Downs but could not respond. I knew Sara would be upset, but hearing that scolding tone in her voice made it all too real for me. I could lose this gig and potentially ruin my career because I was high and hostile. What have I done?

"Get up." Downs said again, more forcefully. "We need to get you into a cell. It's already been a long night."

I lifted my head to Downs standing in front of me. The look on my face must have been pathetic enough to draw some empathy out of the officer. He shook his head and pursed his lips like a disappointed father would do to his incorrigible son. "Pull yourself together, man." He said quietly. "We'll hold you here until you can see a judge. You'll be all right."

"And when will that be?" I sounded indignant to my ears. Downs didn't bother to tell me.

"Let's go." He said. With sharp brown eyes, he looked down at me. Suddenly my big body felt small and helpless. My legs wobbled a little as I got to my feet. A strong wave of nausea passed through me. I thought I would upchuck again. It passed as quickly as it came. I looked around the crowded room, hoping to find a familiar face in the sea of the accused and justice—someone to vouch for me. Only strangers looked back at me with the same lost glance about their futures. "This way." Downs ordered.

In a quiet, fearful, intoxicated haze, I followed Downs out of another door that led to a long, white hallway. At the end was a large steel door that looked as impenetrable as a bank vault. I flinched at the sight of it. Imagining myself on the other side of that door. The white corridor seemed to lengthen with every step closer to its end. My stomach clenched so hard that I buckled inward and nearly fell over. Downs glanced back at me over his shoulder, then turned to face me when he noticed I'd stopped. He stood over my bowed body. I could feel the sting of his glare on my back. I didn't dare to look up.

"What's the problem now, boy?"

"I'm not feeling right. My stomach. It aches. I think I might need a doctor." I felt the weight of what seemed like another man's body keeping me prostrate. Then a hot, cold breath waft over my shoulder, shooting into my nostrils like smoke blown into my face. I spun around so quickly that I fell back, crushing my cuffed hands. Pain shot through my arms like lightning. There was no one in the empty behind us. And we were at the far end of the long hallway.

When did we travel so far?

I looked up at Officer Downs, punching in a code at the keypad next to the mighty door. When it opened, it released a sound like a million men gasping for clean air while drowning in a single pool.

"Get your ass up off the floor." Downs ordered. "Welcome to your new quarters, choirboy." He reached one big black hand down to pull me up from the floor by my arm. I struggled a little with him, still looking back for whatever held me down. I found nothing. Yet I could feel a behavior looming in the hall. A presence just like the one in the patrol car. It seemed to be all around me now. A stale dank sent discharged into the hall from the shadowy grey room on the other side of the threatening door. I noticed that the holding cell was considerably more significant than the booking room as I scrabbled to my feet, looking inside.

Down's face gave no sign he felt the frigid air, smelled the tomb's rank odor, or—more importantly—sensed the menacing presence looming about the hall. There was nothing in his stone-brown eyes to indicate anything other than duty. A hint of disappointment stared back at me from those brown eyes, too. An annoyance there too. Another long night on the job dealing with trouble-makers like the one I'd become that night.

"Your cell is the open door on the other side of the room." Downs said somberly. "I'll follow you in and un-cuff you at the entrance." He paused. Then asked, "You alright?" And there was the hint of concern I was missing in his voice.

"Can't imagine you'd care," I said. Still stubborn. Reluctant to trust.

"You're right, Songbird." He grinned down at me. "But I'll mention to the guards that you requested a medical visit. They might help you in the morning if you make it through the night."

"Don't waste your breath," I said through clenched teeth and hot pride. I straightened and stepped past him in my best efforts to avoid a wobbling or a stumbling over. "It'll pass, I'm sure."

"I'll mention it anyway." Downs said as he crept behind me.

The circular room was dimly lit and half the size of a high school gymnasium. The walls were white too. Along the walls were more steel doors. These with tiny square windows just below the top frames. The doors had no hinges. They slid into the wall to let prisoners in and out of the small rooms.

Faces peaked at me through those windows as I walked by the cells. Some men shouted lude remarks at me that were too muffled behind the doors to understand the words. Other men made obscene gestures with their fingers and their faces. A few men stared back at me with sullen, sunken glares of disappointment as if they expected someone to save them from the misery deep in the walls.

Downs tapped me on the shoulder, veering me away from crashing into a long metal table in the center of the room. It looked like a menacing caterpillar petrified on its back. The stools stuck out from the sides as if waiting to inflict severe pain on the sitter.

The presence followed us into the larger room. It was by my side, whispering words I could barely make out into my ear. I had finally resolved that it was the drugs in my system, having an incredible effect on my senses. Or I was losing my mind as some spiritual karma for what I had done to Jamie in the streets. Those were the only choices that made sense of what was happening inside my head.

Standing at the entrance to my cell, I saw a moonbeam slash the darkness of the tiny room, spreading out along the floor. A barefoot was in the light as if someone were sitting on the right-side bunk. The skin of the appendage was an inhuman gray color, nearly camouflaged by the moonlight. A slight gasp escaped me as the cuffs freed my wrists, causing my shoulders to fall. I couldn't move any further inside. The foot was still, too. As if waiting for me.

"Get inside." Downs ordered.

"There's someone in there," I stated.

"Not until you get inside." Downs gave me a shove forward that pushed me past the threshold. When I turned to him, he was already walking away from the cell. Then the door whooshed shut. Through my tiny window, I watched Officer Downs leave the holding cell. It felt like I had lost my last fan.

I found two empty metal-framed bunks on either wall in the ten-by-eleven cell. A toilet with a sink above it between the beds and a tiny sliver of a window just above the bathroom area. The silver light shined through the window and spread out along the floor like a thin movie projector beam. There was no gray foot in the light. Even the ominous presence I felt seemed to slip from the surrounding air. Finally, alone with my pain, I dropped to my knees on a cold, cemented floor. I wept like a scolded child.

MY PRIVATE HELL

Ж

On the floor in the narrow light of the moon, I sobbed softly to the solid grey walls that only held back the sound of my cries. Just a few days ago, my voice soared through the acoustic walls of the opera house during dress rehearsal. I was high then. I had smoked a joint with Jamie before he drove me to the theatre. We argued then. I don't even remember what about. My throat felt dry and rough. I could still sing the role without a hitch. I just needed tea. It seemed then no matter what I did to my instrument, I'd never lose the gift—my gift. No matter the abuse, I was always ready to sing for all engagements. Without a warm-up, the voice, always there, ready to inspire, in perfect pitch and impeccable tone, made my competition fearful of its power.

As I tried to holler or scream in agony that night in my cell, no musical sound would escape me. My hand clasped my throat in a panic as I tried to hum a bar or two from my opening aria. Nothing came out of my dry mouth. I leaped to my feet, crashing into the toilet/sink. Frantically, I pumped the nozzle at the head of the sink, cupping my hands under the spigot to fill them with water to drink. I drank down the lukewarm liquid, trying to moisten my throat. I smacked the nozzle again to fill my cupped hands. The water was a little colder, but not by much. I gulped it down. Then I tried to hum again, and nothing came out of my mouth. I wet my face with the cool water, hoping it would wake me from this nightmare. I straightened and stared out the slither of a window; I tried another hum. This time, a raspy hiss of a sound pushed forward from my lips. It was a far cry from my episodic aria, but something was still there to work with.

"Thank you," I whispered, shutting my eyes. To whom I said it too, I couldn't be sure, then. I was just grateful.

I saw the world I had just come from through the skinny window. A bullseye view of the exact spot where the fight had occurred was right outside, within plain view. I spot a small light that seems to grow in the same place where I had beaten Jamie on the corner outside the Windbro apartments. The light grew until it became the shape of a cross burning and then turned to a man on fire and moving violently, as I imagined I did while I fought my lover on that same street corner. Then it stopped.

The burning figure turned toward my cell window and seemed to look up at me from the half-mile between us. He burned there in quiet destruction, not moving. I could feel his eyes on me despite the distance. And the more I stared into him, the more precise he became. The hypnotic flames around him captivate and delight my senses. There was no question in my mind. This site was an illusion. But my mind felt utterly lucid, free of whatever drug Jamie had tricked me into smoking that night. The burning man outside my window sobered me for a moment.

"Hey..." I heard another man's voice behind me, husky with a heavy bass. I turned as if I knew the voice. Then I remembered the gray foot before I entered the cell. The fear struck me. I heard a voice that wasn't my own.

A man I didn't see blew a billow of smoke into my face. He worked quickly. I fell back onto the metal bunk and sunk into it, slumped against the wall behind me. I fell into a horrifying nightmare.

A younger version of myself at thirteen. I stood in the crook of a glossy black grand piano on the stage of a dark recital hall I vaguely remember from too long ago. I nervously sang the verses of *Caro Mio ben,* a famous art song used by voice teachers to teach singers vocal range and melodic structure. The chairs in the hall were empty. The hood of the grand piano raised, and my hand rests tightly in the ledge's nook as I belt out the song. My mother accompanied me on piano. A spotlight shone down on me as a fake sun that produced more heat than was bearable in my tight navy blue suit bought years earlier for special occasions like the one we were preparing for. I was burning up while I sang as if my life depended on it. My grip on the piano ledge was so tense my knuckles were nearly white. My voice felt coarse and overworked.

Mama didn't enjoy breaks. She found them to be a waste of precious time. So, she didn't give many of them during our lessons. Especially when there was a show to prepare for, I could feel her eyes glaring at the back of my head and imagined her warning me about my posture and to remember to breathe deeply at the rest, to take in plenty of air for the long musical phrases of the Italian art song. My diction was always lousy back then. She constantly reminded me I wasn't singing pop songs or gospel music but the classics. I should make the language sound natural like I'd been born and raised in Italy.

Those eyes felt like pitchforks stabbing my back. I sweat incessantly. But then my voice just stopped. No sound would come out of my mouth, though I mouthed the words while Mother played on, seeming not to notice or care that I wasn't singing. The piano sounded muffled like I was wearing earplugs or listening to the melody through a wall. Mother played on without me. Then she laughed the most sinister cackle I'd never heard come from her before father murdered her. This was strange because I expected her to leap from the piano stool and strike me across the face as she did throughout other sessions when we were alone and training. She never thought I took my gift seriously enough. I thought she was jealous of my talent, expecting more from me.

In this dream, the laughter seemed to fit her true nature. The poignant way it stabbed at the surrounding air. With the start of a new screech, the volume and length of the laughter would elevate, striking my inner ear with a sharp, blistering pressure.

In the dream, young me curled away from the howling while—I—the dreamer in the cell, cringed on the steel slab I slept on. She began playing the song in a mad fury. Her body was still like a dummy. Only her hands and fingers danced along the ivory keys. The piano rocked so hard that the stick holding the lid open shook loose and crashed down on my hand. Mother played on, laughing wildly. Playing too fast for any singer to keep up. I couldn't feel the pain of the lid on my crushed hand.

I looked at my mother in desperation and found her at the head of the piano with a noose made of bedsheets around her neck. The rest of the line hoisted in the air into the rafters of the stage lights as something pulled at the line of tied sheets. Mama floated above the piano as it played the song without the aid of her fingers. She moved them as if still playing in her absence like the keys were still under her fingers. The music finally stopped. Her fingers quiet too.

With my right hand jammed in the hood of the grand piano, I watched my mother's body dangle above. Slowly, she lost her breath. Her feet shuffled above the piano hood as her toes tapped on it as quick water drops in a bucket after a fast rain. Then, she was motionless. Before I could scream, a burst of applause rose from the empty chairs. The applause was so loud it would have woken the dead.

It hurled me out of the bunk and sent me crashing to the cement floor with what felt like a firm kick in my back. The fermented odor of piss and shit mixed with pine cleaner wafted through my nose, snatching me out of the dream. I looked at the bunk I fell asleep on, expecting to find someone there. There was no one. But something was in my cell. I could feel its presence all around me.

Where the moonbeam shone the evening before, now quietly replaced by the dawn of another day, that light pushed the dark presence into a corner of the white cell. I was alone again.

VISITORS

Ж

The pale, florescent bar of light hanging from the ceiling of my cell flickered three times before coming to life. An electrical buzzing current ran through the line like a fly stuck in a jar. It encouraged a slight ache at the base of my skull that shot through my head like a speeding train. I got up from the floor and went to the faucet to douse my face with lukewarm water. I felt as high as I did when they threw me into the cell. A little less drunk, but the fog hadn't left my brain. In the middle of taking a piss, the large metal entrance to my cell slid open with a thunderous noise behind me. More pain shot through the back of my skull and down my spine this time. A little stream of urine missed the toilet and soaked the bottom of my pant leg when I turned to see what was happening outside the cell.

"Breakfast!" said a loud voice over the intercom system. A few men caught me zipping up my pants as they passed by. One guy lingered around my entrance like he was looking for something or someone other than me. "Let's make this day easy, fellas." The intercom voice commanded. My feet felt cemented to the floor. Walking out of my cell door into the terrifying new circumstance would make things all too real for me. I wasn't sure I was ready to face the day.

The consequence if I didn't—I knew—would be more significant.

I stepped toward the door, then took another two and a few more. I was in the main room. Disgruntled inmates took most of the stools at the upside-down centipede in the middle of the massive white room. They were shoveling dollops of grey mush dragged from the bowls before them into their mouths. I watch them swallow the breakfast quickly. A few men looked up at me as I passed, heading for the last two empty stools on the corner end. The corners were empty on both sides of the inverted centipede.

On the tabletop in front of me was a bowl of gray stuff that looked like twice warmed-over oats from days ago. Beside the bowl was a carton of chocolate milk, like the ones you get in grade school during lunchtime. And there was an apple. To one side of the fruit was a large rotting mass turning black from age. The rest of it looked candy red and ripe enough to eat. I'm allergic to apples.

My stomach grumbled. A sharp sting etched across my gut. I clutched at it secretly, then sat down. The stool was too small for my ample ass and poked at my sit bones. I pulled the bowl closer to me to examine the oats. Like Neil Armstrong's moon flag, the white plastic spoon stuck out of the gray mound.

"What you need to do is shovel it in and swallow to keep from getting the taste on your tongue." I heard a husky voice say from across the table. I didn't see anyone sit down across from me when I sat down. "This shit'll ruin your taste buds for weeks if you let it graze your tongue."

A white man with red hair and a goatee to match sat across from me. He was rather large with upper body muscles. His pale skin was like buttercream. Spots of cinnamon freckles sprinkled around his cheeks. He wore a broad smile between those puffy cheeks that seemed welcoming in the white laboratory-like room. But in his menacing green eyes was a hint of mischief I'd seen on many men before.

My cheeks got hot. If I were a white boy, I'm sure they'd have been as fire-red as his hair. I'm also sure I had to pick my jaw up from the tabletop. He was handsome and rugged. The way I like my men. Something wouldn't let me speak, though. Then, his face was familiar to me. He was the boy from the booking room talking to the cop, the young man who looked misplaced in time. Only this man looked like his older brother. The shapes that made up his features seemed to shift and blur in front of me. I blinked hard, hoping to find focus. His face sharpened again, but not exactly the way it started. Now, they were steady.

"You'd better eat up," the white man said. "It's going to be a long day waitin' for nothin' till lights out." The southern twang in his voice made him sound like something out of a cartoon.

"I'm getting out of here today." I finally said.

"Quiet inmate." An authoritative voice said over the intercom. "Your mouth should be full of oats and not talking shit."

What's the difference? I almost said until I saw a sharp look of warning graze the face of my new breakfast companion. Looking down at the bowl of crusted mush, I reached for the chocolate milk instead.

"Better save that for the chaser, boy." He whispered. "Scarf that shit down like I told you. You won't see another meal till noon, and that's a long way off. Eat up."

I didn't like the chastising tone in his voice. And I certainly didn't like some white man calling me 'boy' to my face. My stomach growl made me decide not to press the issue and do as he said. A carton of milk wouldn't hold me over until the next meal. However, this white man was getting ahead of himself with our friendship; I couldn't deny that he was right.

With a fast peek down the long table, I got a better view of my fellow inmates. They quietly shoveled spoonfuls of gray matter into their mouths like they hadn't been fed in days. All of them looked hungry for more than morning nourishment. Most men looked like they hadn't shaved in days or bathed longer than that. It surprised me to find more white faces than black around the table. The natural segregation was evident as in any other establishment. All the white men assembled in one section of the table—more towards the center—while the few men of color were at the far end of the table. None of them seemed to know one another. They just looked more comforted by faces that looked like their own as they ate. I was suddenly worried about sitting across the table from a white guy.

A sharper pain etched across my stomach.

"Fine." I sheepishly resigned to myself. I picked up a spoonful of oats and shoveled it into my mouth. I swallowed hard and took another and then some more. I closed my eyes, imagining the meal was fresh poached eggs or one of Sara's famous spinach and Swiss omelets. I heard soft laughter coming from the other side of the table. It sounded like the laughter I'd heard the night before in the cop car. It frightened my eyes open.

My ginger-haired, freckled friend from the past was gone.

I looked around the room, trying to find him. Other inmates were moving away from the table. Discarding their empty bowls in the trash bin at the center of the room. I snatched the carton of chocolate milk from the table, opened it up, and drank it in one gulp. When I finished, I felt another sharp pain attack my gut, then disbursed just as quickly as it came. I thought I would vomit. I'm glad I didn't.

There were four of us left at the table. A bald white man with a long torso and big arms. He ate his food slower than the others and appeared to be enjoying the meal. A shorter, Hispanic man sat closer to me— three seats down. He could have been Native American or Mexican. I couldn't be sure. He got up from the table with a short storm, slammed his trash in the bin with a heavy dunk, and walked off into a cell to the right of my own. His long black hair fell to his butt and whipped behind him like a black wave.

At the far end of the table was an older black man. He had to have been in his sixties or even older. His tan, wrinkled face was buried beneath a mane of coarse white hair. Those sharp brown eyes were familiar to me. He had been chanting over his food since breakfast started. I heard him in the background but thought nothing of it until it was the only sound left in the large white room. He hadn't touched his food. The chant reminded me of a song I'd heard in childhood, but I couldn't put my finger on the tune's name. He raised his head and ceased his chant to look over at me. Those brown eyes pierced through me like needle pricks. Then he smiled at me. "Don't trust it." He said with a swift smile. His voice was low, but I heard the words clearly when they came again. "Don't trust it."

"What?" I asked.

The white man with the long torso in the center of the table leaped from his stool, snatched up his trash, and slammed it into the bin with such force that the rotting fruit made a sizable thud as it hit the bottom of the can. The man stomped off to a cell at the far left of the dormitory.

I was nervous enough to scream, but I held it inside. My heart raced. These men are all mad. In all my 'get high' times, I'd ended up in strange places; I never pictured I'd see the inside of a holding cell. When did it get so bad? How in the world did I let my addiction take me this far?

The old black man moved in closer to me, just enough for me to get a better look at the face buried beneath all that nappy, coarse white hair. He looked more familiar to me; only it couldn't be who I thought it was. That man was dead. Years had gone by now. But this old man resembled what his corps would be after all these years. "Don't trust it." He said again. That swift smile again. Just like a jazz skip. This time, as he moved closer to me, he wore a maniacal grin and wild in his eyes. I waited for the guards to call out to him over the intercom from the viewing booth. They said nothing.

The old man burst into a looney-tooned laughter right in front of my face. Bits of spittle sprinkled me. The laughter changed to a lion-like roar. Holding my stare, he walked past me and around the table to exit into the cell next to mine without looking back at me. Laughing that raucous roar even after he was inside his cell, out of view.

I was alone at the table. The doors to the cells were still open to the tiny worlds of the inmates inside. Most of the cells had two inmates who didn't seem to know one another because they avoided each other in the cramped space. I was glad to be one of the lucky ones to have a cell to myself. Heaven only knows what they would have thrown in there with me.

The guard's station was glassed into a rectangular room at the far wall by the entrance of the holding cell. I could see five guards in the space dressed in brown-bag-colored uniforms and some with black caps on their heads. They watched from a far enough distance to let a good fight break out in the central area before deciding to come into the only entrance to the cell and break it up. If someone hadn't committed a serious crime like murder or assault before he was arrested, the likelihood he would – just trying to stay alive in this place–is increased by double, I'm sure. The criminals looked hardened, and the guards looked like angry bricks waiting to be thrown at any glass house. Desperation etched in shame was written over every face in the holding cell. I wondered if I looked the same.

I got up from the table to toss my trash and take a last look for the Ginger Boy that startled me at breakfast. I still couldn't find him. A man couldn't just vanish from a holding cell.

"Stay where you are, inmate." The intercom voice ordered just as I turned from the trash bin, heading back to my cell. I turned around and looked toward the window of the guard's booth and found a round guard who filled his brown bag uniform with his whole fleshy body. He pointed at me. Then, he put up his open palm as a signal to stop. I stood by the trash bin, waiting. Some other inmates huddled at their open cell doors to look at whatever action was about to go down. I was nervous enough to fill my pants with breakfast. All kinds of ideas sprung to my mind. I feared the officers would strip-search me before the other men. I don't remember Officer Downs giving me a patdown when he brought me in.

When the entrance to the holding cell opened, another brown uniformed guard entered. He was tall and broad and wore a service cap covering his face's top half. His mouth was big. He pointed at me and said, "You! Come with me."

I don't know why I looked back to my cell, but from where I stood, I had a bullseye view of the inside, straight to the narrow window. I saw my Ginger Man standing in the cell with his back to me, looking out of that slither of a window. One broad white arm propped against the wall. His right leg crossed his left. My view of him was gone when the doors slammed shut in unison.

The sudden realization of a cellmate was a distraction as I followed the guard down several long white hallways lined with steel doors with keypads and no doorknobs. I remember going down a flight of stairs before we came to another white hall with fewer doors. These doors were open and led to tiny rooms with what looked like visiting stations, glassed off on one wall where a lonely chair faced the window. The rooms were dark, even with a small light in the ceiling.

My mind was still cloudy. What had Jamie put in those joints? Under normal circumstances, I'd be hungover by this hour—if I were awake—reaching for another joint or a drink to even me out so I could deal with whatever the day had prepared for me. That morning, it felt like the night had never stopped, like I was sifting through a long dream in real time.

I nearly ran into the guard when he suddenly stopped at an entrance to one of the tiny rooms. He turned to me and dismissingly waved me inside.

"Sit in the chair and wait." He told me. The brim of his hat cast a shadow over his face. It was impossible to see his eyes. He was slightly taller than my six feet and one inch. I had to look up to see him. No matter how hard I squinted to make something out, I found no recognizable characteristics on his face.

"What's in there?"

"You have a visitor." He said. "Get inside. Sit down. If no one is there, you wait. I'll be back for you." I never saw a mouth move the entire time he gave his instructions. This stopped me from asking who had come for me or how much time I had with them.

What was happening inside my head?

He put me inside the room with a less-than-gentle shove and closed the door behind me. I stood there momentarily, dreading the reality I knew was waiting for me. I tilt my head back to release a colossal sigh, trying to pull myself together. I smelled the sweet, familiar fragrance of a shampoo I'd known for many years. The brand she couldn't live without. I had gone out in a Manhattan snowstorm to get a bottle when she was in the last trimester of her pregnancy with our little girl. Watermelon and raspberry lemon filled the small space as they did our bathroom just days before Mya was born. That scent filled every room she entered.

"Sara," I whispered. Just saying her name brought renewed faith. I walked to the chair and sat down.

I found my wife sitting in the chair on the opposite side of the plexiglass window. Her long, thick, brown hair was like a murky river streaming down her delicate shoulders. Those steel-blue eyes in her thin, angular face were like ice picks. The disappointment was written in the scowl she wore. Frowning at her forehead and pursing her supple red lips. Even angry with me, she was picturesque. Her glare reminded me of the mess I had made or our agreement about our marriage. I had become a burden the more successful we became. I wanted to cry. But what good would tears do? She had seen me that way too many times for tears even to matter. I wanted to say 'sorry,' but it meant nothing to her since nothing would change.

"I talked to Danial this morning." She said through the tiny holes in the center of the plexiglass window.

"When can they get me out of here?"

"They can't." She lowered her eyes. "The company is set to throw in your understudy if you aren't at rehearsal tonight."

Miles Palmer. A squeaky voice tenor. Hard on the ear. He swore he'd do the role in blackface to keep the integrity of the character. The audience would walk out at the top of Otello's opening aria if he were to replace me.

"He's more than ready." Sara continued. "He's fantastic and has played the role in the past for a company in Italy. If your voice weren't God's blessing, they would have given him the role at the start."

"You think he's better than me?"

"You're killing yourself with your bad habits. What is it with you, Cameron? I thought we agreed…"

"I know," I said. I lowered my eyes. "I'm sorry."

"This will get out to the local press." She said. "It will ruin you with every opera house."

"I know."

"I don't think you do, Cameron." The pity in her voice made me look up at her again. "You're an addict. It's time to face up to that."

"You're overthinking this…"

"I'm not," Sara said. There were tears trapped in the lower lid of her eyes she wouldn't let drop. "Do you even know what happened to your friend?"

"Did someone talk to you?"

"No one told me anything. I was hoping I'd get the truth from you." Her eyes narrowed, and those trapped tears ran streams down her cheeks. I wanted to hold her. Tell her I'd make this all right again. But I wasn't sure that I could. "I don't know anything about your lovers. I'm here for you. For Mya."

"Sara, we agreed…"

"I know what we agreed to." She said, wiping the tears away. "You're still high from last night. I can see it in your face. They don't notice, but I always know."

"I need your help to get out of here. I'm already losing my grip." I said. "I need you to talk to the company on my behalf. Miles' performance will end the show before the first intermission. The public is expecting me."

"Do you think the company doesn't notice what you are?" Sara's back stiffened. She sat upright and grew to fill in the space around the window. "There's been talk." She said. "Lots of talk about you and the drinking and the drugs. Our marriage. Your affairs…"

"People should mind their own business."

"This show is our business, Cameron." She said in a sharp, penetrating tone.

"I hear the things they say about us," I said. "To hell with what they say. We know the truth, and we chose this life—for Mya. Let them say what they want. We hit that stage. We get the job done. The people are satisfied. All is forgiven—swept under the rug. Like always." I put my open palm against the plexiglass. She stared further into me, looking for something I didn't think she believed she could find. I prayed she felt my desperation. "Sara. Help me get to opening night. Talk to Danial."

"I want you to promise me something."

"Anything."

"The addictions end today." She said. "No drugs, booze, sex... men. No more of it. We focus on what is best for our family and leave the disgrace behind. Can you promise me that?"

I was silent longer than I should have been. I wanted to lie. I wanted to tell her I could give it all up. I believed by doing that, our lives would go back to normal. I had complete control of my life before that night of the fight. I was under a tremendous amount of pressure. And seeing my lover kissing someone else right in front of me was the last straw. I couldn't hold it together any longer. This addiction stuff was crazy talk. I had a few drinks. I smoked a few blunts. I lost control.

"You can't do it." She said. "Can you?"

My hand slid down the plexiglass window, defeated.

"I can promise…" I said.

Her ice-blue glare was hard enough to break the glass between us.

"What can you promise?"

"I promise to do my best to stay away from my addictions. I'll stay focused." I said. I wanted to believe it. "Help me convince the company they need to get me out of here and back on that stage where I belong."

I heard a deep, menacing rumble of laughter coming from the corner of my side of the visiting booth. It mocked me as if it knew that I couldn't shake my demons by opening night. I probably had no intention of ever shaking them. I said whatever it would take to get me out of that county jailhouse. I knew I didn't belong there. I shook the laughter off my back. The door on my side of the visiting room opened as the guard entered.

"Time's up!" He said. The inside of my mouth felt as dry as hot summer dirt. My heart hurt. My stomach clenched and cramped.

"You look like hell warmed over, Cameron," Sara said, with the first signs of sympathy in her voice.

"I'll take care of me in here," I said. "Help me get out of this place today, Sara. Talk to the company."

She got up from her chair, backing away from the window as if looking at a stranger. "I'll do what I can." She said, almost inaudibly, before leaving the room without looking back.

I waited for the door to close entirely on her side—the free side—before I got up from my chair. I'm not sure what I was waiting for. The laughter came at me again. At first, it sounded like it was in my head. But then I heard its menacing cackle grow into a robust holler. Filling the room with its sinister music. The guard shouted at me again. I didn't try to understand what he said. I followed the murmuring sound of his voice out of the visiting area, back into the icy white corridors lined with the steel doors of imprisonment.

Sara's leaving solidified my circumstance. I thought I'd wake up that morning hungover. They'd release me with a slap on the wrist. I'd be in my soft bed in my hotel room, sleeping it off until rehearsal later that night.

The rage I unleashed on Jamie blazed back into my memory like wildfire. I watched myself throwing big, angry fists against his face. Thrusting his head to the ground. The throbbing in my knuckles reminded me of how hard I hit. How did I get so angry? That cop didn't check his breathing. He should have checked his breathing!

"You know where to find your place." The guard said, waking me from my thoughts. We were standing at the open entrance of the holding cell again. I didn't remember a single step we took to get there.

I walked inside and was met with the same peeping heads in the tiny square windows of some individual cell doors. They seemed elated that I was back. One man smiled and nodded as if he had bet something on my return and won big.

My cell door was closed. I saw my Ginger Man from the breakfast table that morning through the window. His back to the door. Standing just as I left him to take my visit as if he hadn't moved during my time with Sara. His black cargo pants held him like a new layer of skin. His white T-shirt was just as tight, with the short sleeves rolled up to show off his thick, muscled arms in full alabaster glory. His red hair seemed to have a wicked dance to the peak of his flat-top head. He stared out the slithered window. One forearm pressed to the wall. His forehead rested on his fist.

I looked around to be sure I was at the correct cell door. It seemed too soon to have a celly. I hadn't been gone long.

The door opened. He didn't move an inch then, but I jumped back at the shock of seeing him in full view. His presence brought a stillness to the cell. I felt I needed permission to enter.

"What are you waiting for, inmate?" The voice said over the loudspeaker. "Get in your cell!" The mechanical blast of noise snatched me from my trance. Timid steps led me inside. I stood just a foot from the entrance to let the door slam shut behind me. I shuttered at the sound. My cellmate still didn't move. His stillness was haunting.

"You'll get used to those slamming doors in due time." He said. His body was like an enormous cobra about to strike. His back to me. It seemed like he hadn't said a single word that I heard him speaking in my mind.

CELLYS COLLIDE

Ж

As a young man growing into my sexuality, I'd consistently recognized an insatiable affinity for stocky, muscular white men. The dangerous types. The construction worker or delivery truck driver with a desire for the company of black boys who respect their privacy and feed their indulgences. Such a man had taken advantage of this desire years back. When my parents died, my brother committed suicide sometime later; Sara and I were married. Mya was born. I believe the husky white man was a hustler, but I never knew for sure. We'd met on the street one night in Greenwich Village. I was drunk and horny. We made out in an alley across the street from the piers. I gave him money. And we'd meet regularly to do it all over again—in a park or a side street, and once in a hotel room, I'd used the family's rent money to pay for. We were so broke back then, but I didn't care. The morning after our hotel encounter, it all ended quietly. I woke and found all the money gone from my wallet, along with my credit card. I kept a slip of paper in the wallet with the PIN number on it. I never saw that man again. But the desire to hold a man like him again lingered long after the betrayal.

"Welcome home, Sweet Cheeks." That scratchy tone and country twang in my new Celly's voice was more profound than his back portrayed. It was rich but as hollow as an echo.

"Who are you?" I could finally ask. My voice rasped and exhausted as if I had been singing all day.

"Your celly, Sweet Cheeks." He turned away from the window to face me. "You don't remember me?" He reminded me of that hustler years ago, though I knew it couldn't be him. Those envious green eyes and that devil's grin gave me the impression that I was looking at an old friend. The chill in the room reminded me that in places like this, one had no friends.

"At breakfast—this morning—" I said.

"That's right. Looks like you comin' around." He smirked and slapped his thigh. "For a black boy, you sure as hell lose color quick." I noticed the buckle of his black leather belt was a Confederate flag design. I flinched slightly and hoped he didn't see me see it. He'd have to stop calling me 'boy,' considering. He quit laughing suddenly, then sunk a thumb into his jeans behind the belt buckle to cover the flag with his hand. His chin sunk into his chest. He mumbled his next question.

"What's the matter with you, boy?" He looked up at me again. I felt my face get hot. "Look like you never seen a honkey before today. You even from the U.S. of A?"

"Don't call me that."

"What?" He questioned with a grin. "Boy?"

"I don't want to hurt you."

"I don't want to hurt you either... boy." He paused. His white smile broke any tension that momentarily rose between us. "Man." He said, smiling. Then he burst into laughter again and fell out on the iron cot braced against the right-side wall. I didn't know what I should do. I thought about returning to the door and banging so hard to get the guards' attention. Tell them they locked a black man in a holding cell with a racist.

Whose brilliant idea was that?

"Listen here, Sweet Cheeks," he casually said, "if me and you don't find a common ground during our stay here in this tiny space, one of us is gonna have hell to pay. And I hear the devil has got some high fuckin' fees. I don't mean you no harm. And I'm thinking this is your first time in the pokey. You want to get out of here with everything intact. Am I on the right road so far?"

I shook my head. I was still contemplating losing my shit at the cell door.

"So, how's about me and you agree to be civil to one another for the duration of our stay?" He offered. "That sound good to you, Sweet Cheeks?"

"Don't call me that either," I said and turned away from him to look out the window in the door. The guards were laughing and talking at their post. Looking free and happy. "My name is Cameron." I turned back to him, and my mind must have been playing tricks on me. For a moment, my celly was gone. Then, in a wink, he was there again, easing deeper into the iron cot, pushing his back against the gray wall. After a hesitation, I put my hand out to him like this was the beginning of a job interview. "Cameron Grime." He didn't take it.

"I'm not in the habit of shaking hands in lockdown, Cameron Grime." He said, looking down at his grinding hands, fingers crisscrossed, thumbs winding while his big forearms sat on his casual thighs. "My Christian name is Ivan. But they call me Nail in places like this."

My brow raised in comic wonder. "Is that right?" I said. I wanted to laugh but thought against it. Growing up in Westchester County, New York, I was never much of a street fighter. My older brother and I would wrestle around the house. He taught me a few moves. I could hold my own against this 'Nail' if it came down to it. I had no intention of testing that theory out, though. I let him have his way about him. I sat down on the bunk I woke up on that morning.

"What they got you in here for? Drugs?" He asked. I could hear the prejudiced assumption beneath the words. And I guess he was right.

"A fight," I said.

"Oh, really?" He said through a sly grin. "With who? Your boyfriend." Right again.

"Watch it," I said. I looked up at him. We half smiled at one another.

"You was drinkin'?"

"I was."

"Doin' drugs too, huh?"

"What are you–working for the D.A.'s office?"

"You were high as hell." He said through that grin again, a little louder that time. "You must have put some kind of hurtin' on that boy if they hauled your black ass up in the poky."

"What do you know about anything?"

"I know if you killed your little boyfriend, they gonna lock your black ass up in a cage quicker than you can flick your Bic. That, I do know, boy?" This time, he cackled like a burning hot crow.

"I told you not to call me that." I raised up from the wall and pulled myself to the edge of my iron cot. I could feel the blood rush to my cheeks.

"Oh, so yousa tough guy, huh? A hot-head, badass, muthafuckin' black boy?"

I got up from my cot. I was towering over him. There was little space between us.

"You took my bunk last night." He said without even looking up at me. He just sat there, twiddling his thumbs like I wasn't even standing there.

"There was no one in here last night."

"I was right there on that bunk behind you when they hauled your pretty black ass in here around three in the morning." He said. "You were so gone you didn't even notice me."

"I was alone in this cell."

"Cardo Mio ben..." He sang. His voice turned the classic tune into a country western song sung by a campfire. I could almost hear the guitar.

I was alone in this cell when I woke up this morning. How could he have been there last night? How could he know I sang that song in my dream? Who is this freak? There was no one here. The memory of the gray foot in the moonlight came to me. I pushed the thought out of my mind. I remembered that the foot looked dead, attached to something deader. I sat back down on the iron bunk, stunned.

"You got a good voice, Sweet Cheeks." He said. He was having fun now. "Yousa singer?"

"Yes," I said quietly.

"Who's Jamie?"

"What?" The sound of my lover's name leaving his mouth frightened me, so I thought he would tell me something I didn't know but needed to. "How do you know that name?"

"I heard you moaning it out in your sleep." He said.

There was no one in here last night but me.

"Is he the boyfriend you beat up on the street corner last night?"

I didn't answer. But what was my expression saying to him? I couldn't tell.

"There you go gettin' pale again, Sweet Cheeks." Nail said. "You're all right. Your secret's safe with me. What a man do with his backside is his own business. Who am I to judge him for it?" He kept his laughter to himself, staring at his hands like he feared they'd vanish.

What had I said in my sleep? More than I wanted to this jailhouse racist. I looked away from him to gaze into the skinny window. There was a line of blue sky shining through the cold cement wall. I imagined I could taste the crisp air of fall rising.

"Shit! If you don't want to believe I was in here last night, I'll pretend with you." He said. "Even one night out of this cage would be enough for me."

"What are you in here for?" Suddenly, that was all I wanted to know.

"This time?" He said, looking up from his hands. A dangerous joy ignited in his eyes. "Drunk and disorderly." Nail went quiet momentarily, shifting his weight to the right hip, leaning on his elbow, and playing with his hands again. He looked innocent of nothing. "Them cops claim I might have violated somebody. I don't remember nothing like that. I wouldn't do nothing so vial…"

"Violated?" I said. "Like, how?"

"I said I don't remember doin' nothing like that!" His words seemed to shake the cell walls. I pressed on anyway.

"Then," I hesitated, but curiosity won my tongue. "What do you remember?"

He sat up straight in the bunk at the edge closest to me. He waited there, staring into me like he was reading my thoughts or trying to find some clue behind my eyes. "Now, who's workin' for the D. A.'s office?" He asked. "What you need to know about me for?" A clever smirk aroused his face. His shoulders eased as he settled again against the gray wall behind him. For just a moment, he disappeared, then reappeared right before my eyes. Jamie's drugs were still playing tricks on my mind. I could still feel them coursing through my blood. Whatever it was he laced those joints with was riding me hard. It took me to dark places I didn't like to think about. Like mom, Dad, and Russel before we met Mr. Grime and his daughter, Sara. My fake wife. Mother to my fake daughter. My real niece. Pretending everything was picture-perfect.

"I get to drinkin' and lose track of my actions." Nail said quietly. I barely heard him through my fog.

"I know how that is."

"Do you?"

"Yeah."

"Nothin' 'bout you smell like an addict to me."

"I wouldn't call myself an addict—"

"Yup! There it is!" He said, pointing a 'gotcha' index finger at me while raising a brow. He let his legs fall open and relax. They looked like two heavy logs from a thick baby oak tree. I had to turn away to hide my interest.

He pushed away from the wall and let his heavy black boots hit the floor before him. Both feet landed like feathers shaken from a crow's back. Then he slapped my thigh with too much force in his right hand. I sat up off the wall to face him. We were close enough to kiss or bite each other. I could smell his breath and body odor. At first, it was like apples fresh off the tree. Then, in an instant, the smell of him changed to rotting meat and earth. I gaged and pulled back. When I looked into his face again, it was morphing in and out of ages — from boyhood to manhood, to elder, back to the boy, back to the man.

I got up from my bunk to look out the window. I didn't know what was happening to me. I feared what would happen if I didn't get out of there. What if I didn't get out? I was just another black man behind a wall of crime. Forget about any show I was supposed to sing in. I violated the law. I disturbed the peace. I may have killed a man.

My lover...

The dull silver-white walls of the main room of the holding cell made it look like a dungeon in a cumulus cloud, aimlessly drifting with the wind. I had been pacing from the window outside to the one in the middle of the door. The toxic mix of mental anguish and a deep desire for freedom overwhelmed my steps. My skin was hot with the sour stench in the air. My skeleton quivered inside me as if lost in a snowstorm.

Why would they put this country bumpkin in my cell?

"Best you relax, Sweet Cheeks," Nail said, just as I forgot he was there. "We'll be stuck together for another night. One of us might get lucky come mornin'."

"There's half the day. It can only be noon—"

"Noon?" Nail said. "It's nearly three in the afternoon. They'll call for dinner soon."

"What happened to three hots', a squat, and a cot?" I complained.

Nail sat up on the bunk to tell me, "As your lockdown representative, I'm here to inform you that shit don't always go like you want it to, in the pokey." He yelled like he'd heckled a failing comic in a crowded comedy house. It thrilled him to bust my spirit. He laughed long and hard at me. It felt like a room full of men. He laid back on the bunk. His smoke-shiny black boots faced me at the foot of the bunk while I stood at the door. He looked like a worn-out Aryan Brotherhood reject from a dying pack of clan hopelessness.

How any man could get through a day in a shithole like this, I did not know. But I managed. Nothing around to distract my thoughts. How could there be rehabilitation?

"Where are you from?" I finally asked Nail.

"Alabama. Tuskegee."

"You still got family down there?"

"All dead."

I couldn't face the inside of the cell anymore. I kept looking into the empty white main room, trying not to stare at the guards in the booth. I only started talking to Nail again because it felt good to speak to someone. My attraction to him had dwindled. Seeing that belt buckle reminded me of the rage that stole my freedom. And a holding cell was definitely not a good place for sex with a white male stranger. "You mean you're the last." I paused. Then, "You never told me your last name—"

"'Cause you don't need to know it." He bit back at me. I turned back to the window. This time, I watched the guards. Their solemn faces looked at nothing on monitors they didn't want to watch—the things we do for money.

"My great granddaddy owned a plantation in Tuskegee." Nail went on. "The family lost it after he died. Sold off most of the lands except a small plot my momma had a trailer on. I was raised up there. I had a brother that died in the war—"

"Which one?" I asked, still watching the guards. It looked like one of them was telling a funny story to the others listening intently. They all laughed. I wish I had heard the story. I forgot I asked Nail a question. My thoughts drifted to imagine Sara talking to Danial about my situation. His long, wide frame standing on the rehearsal stage, rocking on his heels. His salt and pepper hair slicked back to perfection, not a single thread standing out of the glide. He'd have his arms folded with one hand playing with the gray hairs at the tip of his long beard. He'd listen to Sara's sad plea for her broken songbird. Knowing all along there was nothing he would do. Miles would go on in blackface because the show must go on. He rehearsed Miles more than he did me. His excuse was that I was born to play the role. There was nothing he could direct me to do better. I took that as an insult.

He'll nod sympathetically at Sara. Waiting for the moment, he could dig into her with a snide jab about his warning about me when we first met. I was told he was telling company members that he feared I'd pull some prima donna act to inflate the offstage drama of the production. He blamed his fear on my reputation.

Our agent Fay Reynolds—mine and Sara's—went to bat for us on this gig. She pleaded with casting to let us audition together. Even offered to fly them out to New York. That way, we wouldn't have to be away from Mya. We sang for them in an old church in downtown Brooklyn. Mya sat between the agents like she was the most critical person in the room. They loved her. I think that's why they fell in love with us. Not just our voices.

Fay was better than brilliant that night. She earned her fifteen percent.

Sara would need to call Fay as well and explain. Knowing Fay, she'll be in Denver the next thing smoking, ready to raise hell the following day. She'll make them get me out or break me out herself. Thoughts like that comfort me like a warm blanket in winter. It soothed me.

I finally returned to my iron cot, somewhat ready to listen to Nail rattle on about himself. To my surprise, my cellmate must have gotten tired of me and decided to nap. He was curled up in as close to a fetal position as a big man like him could get. I couldn't understand how he could be so casual and comfortable on such a hard surface. Perhaps he'd been there long enough to where his body was used to the stonelike surface. I hoped I'd never get that comfortable.

Laying back on my cot and staring at the ceiling, all I could hear was the great humming sound coming from the daggling fluorescent light on the top. I imagined breaking through the roof into the free, clean air of the real world. I had to close my eyes to float into the freedom of a summer dream.

In real-time, the Fall had settled into the mountains around the city—scenes of trees in their golden-brown glory. Sagging limbs full of transformation began to shrivel like cray paper.

In my daydream, I held on to the new life of spring. Stronger branches flared with green plumage that bathed in the warm, sparkling sunlight. Vibrant wind blowing a warm summer breeze. Beneath my body, I imagined more than an iron cot. Tickling green grass cuddled me in an earthly embrace. I thought I'd lay there for my stay in that jailhouse.

The buzzing from the light turned to a familiar hissed laughter that slowly crept around my ears. Then it grew into its own sound that punished my vision with mocking giggles as if I had no right to dream happy. I clapped my hands over my ears, and the sound seemed to grow inside my head. When I tried to open my eyes, the lids felt sewn shut. With much force, I could finally pry them open to the gray-white misery of my cell. I was staring at the ceiling again.

"Damn drugs," I said.

The loud screeching alarm bell sounded. The cell door slid open. Quickly rising, I got up from my cot and went to the entrance. The other inmates left their cells and headed for the meal table, where white bowls were placed before each stool.

As I walked through the entrance, Nail appeared out of thin air. Bumping into me with enough force to turn me around.

"You'd better get at your lunch before one of those big fuckers takes it for himself." Nail said without even looking my way.

"Where did you come from?"

"What? You think you the only inmate here who gets visitors?"

"I didn't hear you leave."

"You were passed out."

"I... I was resting my eyes." Even I didn't believe the words.

"What's the fuss about?"

"I didn't hear you leave—and you appeared–" I couldn't think of the words that would make sense.

"You're still high, Sweet Cheeks." He said.

He could have been right. It could have been the drugs.

"Go on and git your lunch, Bo—" Our eyes locked before he could speak again. "I'll be here when you get back." He said as if I'd miss him.

"You're not going to eat?"

"I had mines on my way back from my visit. Them bowls been sitting out there for at least five minutes. Your slop's probably cold—long as you been standin' in the doorway." He said. "Ain't nothin' worse than cold jailhouse slop."

"You said I missed lunch."

"Another thing about the pokey," he was laid out on the cot now. It looked like he was slightly floating, less than an inch above it. I relaxed but could feel the tension reverberate through the small cabin. "Criminals lie." He laughed. The hollow sound in his voice sent a chill up my back. He called to me when I turned away from the door.

"I got a surprise for you when you get back in here." I caught a wicked smile grace his face before I walked out of view. I didn't care for more lies. It felt good to be away from his sneaky talk. I couldn't figure out if he was trying to befriend me or find a way to break me. And what for? I didn't know the man. Why couldn't we sit in that cramped cell and not aggravate one another? When I tried to talk civil to that country bumpkin, he turned it into a power struggle. What was I going to do about it? Complain to the guards? How? They made us so secure that they could turn their backs; all we would do was kill each other. The empty cells would be filled up again by the night's end.

As I approached the table, I noticed a few new faces that looked either scared, shitless to move, or hard enough to start a fight. Perhaps they were men I hadn't noticed before, but the table was almost full now. My seat at the end and the one across from it was empty. My stomach gave a hard grumble as I took my seat. The white styrofoam bowl in front of me was filled with, what looked like, a mountain of wet dog dung that was pissed over. Beside the bowl was a small carton of chocolate milk. I was surprised by the aroma as I leaned over the bowl. It was the pleasant and comforting sensation of fresh beef stewed in onions, carrots, and peas in a nice broth. I didn't bother to look down at it again. I closed my eyes and imagined myself at home with my family, having dinner at the kitchen table because Mama had made her beef stew for supper. I scarfed down that meal like a starved man. The taste of meat and veggies mixed in with the thick broth reminded me of a time when all I knew was the love of family, music, harmony, and a home. Before long, that bowl was empty. My stomach was full. My cheeks spread wide across my face. It was then I could feel eyes on me.

When I opened my eyes, I saw in the corner left view the old man from breakfast was staring at me. His long, ratty white hair tussled around his round face. He was sitting on a stool in the middle of the table. His enormous eyes watching me like an old owl from an old tree.

The other inmates at the table quickly devoured their stew as I had. No one seemed not to enjoy the meal except the old man. His bowl was whole, untouched. The white end of the spoon handle stuck up in the center of the bowl. And he was staring at me. For my life, I couldn't tell where I had seen his face before. Only it wasn't the same face. This one is older, ancient, and ancestral.

A few men between us got up from the table, slammed their bowls in the trash, and exited to their holes in the walls. I had the old man in full view now. And he wasn't hiding the fact that he was staring directly into me. I was getting nervous, so I decided to look back at him.

"Don't trust." He said softly. I barely heard him over the chewing, the grunts, and the footsteps moving back to the dorms. But his words were clear. He was across from me, about four seats down to my left. Though his body was thin and lean, it seemed strong enough to rip the table out of the floor despite his age. His presence demanded the room. And I'm sure in his youth, he was a gorgeous black man.

Next to him was a younger brother with long dreadlocks that branched around his husky body like thick vines. His face was black as tar, and it was hard to tell where his skin ended and his hair took over. He looked hardened in the face by whatever streets in America he grew up on. He caught me staring in their direction and stopped eating to look back at me. The disdain in his glare was familiar. Some straight men believe they can spot a Gay man just by looking at him. And they think that all Gay men want them. They live for the intimidation and harbor self-hate for what they recognize in themselves but are afraid to admit. Even the anger is curiosity. He kept his angry eyes on me as he rose from the table, threw out his bowl, and entered his cell. I looked back, and I'm not sure why. Maybe it was because I saw myself in him. I won't deny there was some desire there. More, I wanted to know his anger. Look inside of it a little and find out why it existed.

The old man got up from the table. He was walking to his cell, which was next to mine. As he approached the doorway, Nail appeared there in our cell frame. An intimidating scowl fell over his face when the old man came upon the cell and looked him in the face. He stood eye to eye, looking at Nail for over a minute. From Nail's sly glare, I thought he would smack the old man to the floor with one stroke. Nail looked more scared of the old man. His skin seemed to turn gray, like the barefoot I saw in the moonlight when they dragged me here. Nail broke his staring contest with the old man to look at me with a crazy, wide-eyed grin. He whirled his index finger around his right-side temple and pointed at the old man. I knew I had lost my mind when I noticed the tip of his finger disappear the further it reached outside the cell's doorway.

The old man straightened his spine like a rising lion, ready to strike. Squaring off his stance, he faced Nail full-bodied, looking like he would devour him with some superpower. Like a lamb to a lion, Nail shrunk away from the door frame into the gray of our small space until I couldn't see him anymore.

I looked at the guard station to see if they witnessed what I'd just seen. My eyes met with glaring eyes from two of the six guards in the booth. I looked at the table and noticed that all the men had gone. Even the old man had retreated into his cell.

"If you're done eating, clean up your trash and return to your cell, inmate. I don't want any trouble." The officer said through the loudspeakers. The noise gave me a start. The guards seemed not to exist. I'd forgotten they were there. I got up from the table, threw out my empty bowl, and headed back to my cell. All the while, I could hear the old man whispering, "Don't trust" in my head. The cell doors hissed closed behind me.

Old white head's words lingered through my head while Nail and I lay quietly on our iron cots. He slept through the afternoon while I paced the cell, waiting for the door to open to my freedom. Danial would second-guess his understudy and order the company to take action. He'd realize the strength my presence would make on that stage and his own career, and he'd break. The company would listen to their show director.

The cell door never opened.

I lay down on the iron cot, staring at that ceiling, trying to catch a glimmer of that blue-sky dream I had before. It never came. Only those words from the old man repeating in my head. "Don't trust." He was obviously talking about Nail after that standoff, but what could he mean? I know not to trust a lunatic racist. The warning way he said those words made me too uneasy to sleep. How the hell did they even know each other? Why was any of that a question in my mind?

I got up and went to the window. The sun was going down. The flickering lights playing in the leaves on the trees made the half-mile park between the Capital Building and the courthouse seem like a majestic, magical field. Lockup, where I was, sat behind the courthouse. I'd seen the building several times with Jamie while we cruised the park for drugs. One night, I asked Jamie what it was, and he told me it was part of the museum beside the courthouse. He wasn't sure. But I could see how he got that impression. From the outside, it looked like a castle out of the mid-evil times, only upgraded for the 21st century. Much like any city, Denver hides its seediness behind artistic expression. Vagrants riddled the park—the homeless slept in the brush at night. Drug trafficked and looted by day. From a distance, the park looked like a beautifully structured flower garden of fantasy.

Jamie and I spent countless hours in that fantasy, not even looking for drugs, just enjoying the night when everything was quiet. He and I played games on the steps of the outdoor amphitheater or sat by the fountain of dolphins while making out under the stars in the Denver air's chill. Jamie intrigued me from the first time we met. There was always an adventure in store whenever he would take me away from my work and help me forget I was a singer, a husband, and a father; I never felt worthy enough to be. It wasn't just the drugs that hooked me to him; I needed the adventure. I can't even be sure if I really loved him.

Drifting out of my memories, I turned to check on Nail. I'm not sure why I did. But he was gone from his bunk. Suddenly, my head ached with a tremendous pounding, and my stomach retched. I quickly spun around, gently fell to my knees before the toilet, and wretched a mix of oats and beef stew. I felt dizzy, like I'd been tossed around on a rollercoaster. I broke into cold sweating, and shivers ran all over my body, though I was hot.

Something about the cell had changed, too. I felt transported to a dark cavern. There was the scent of a million dirty men wafting through the air. And I could feel something else in the room that seemed to suck the life out of the cell. I choked. My throat was dry as sandpaper. The presence loomed around me.

This wasn't any drug. They were wearing off. My cravings kicked in as soon as Sara left me that morning. I wanted to smoke whatever Jamie rolled in those joints. Then go back to his place and fuck like wild animals. I craved that passion. I'd feel better, at least for another night.

"You gonna be alright there, Sweet Cheeks?" Nail's voice said above me. I was in a fetal position when I opened my eyes, half under Nail's cot. He was above, looking down at me like a boy on the top bunk at a sleepover. That fire-red hair was dancing around his head against the dangling fluorescent beam dripping from the ceiling.

"Where'd you come from?" I demanded. "Where'd you go?" Hastily getting up from the floor, I felt somewhat better after my upset. I craved the drug, though. I flushed the regurgitated muddy oats down the toilet and took an exhausted seat on my cot. My hips ached. The night was settling in outside the window, and I wondered how the time had passed so quickly. Why am I still here? "You weren't here a minute ago. I looked for you. Your cot was empty. How did you get out of here?" I couldn't believe the desperation in my voice. "Tell me how you got out of here!"

Nail sat still on the bed for a long while, staring at me like I had another head sprouting from my shoulder. From the look on his face, I thought he might alert the guards.

"I think you need to see a doctor, Sweet Cheeks." He said through a small gin. "I been in here gettin' my beauty rest since you came in from lunch. Then you jump down in the shitter up-chuckin' two of your three hots. You sure as hell lose a lot of color when you sick, boy."

"I told you to stop calling me that."

"I fucked up. Shit!" He said. He almost seemed apologetic. "Your fit nearly scared the living shit out of me! I don't want to be caught in no holding cell with a dead man."

"I can't imagine you being afraid of a dead body."

"Dead body's the least of my worries, Sweet Cheeks." He said. "The less interaction I have with them boys dressed in paper bags, the better. I hate them fucks."

"The guards?"

"Them. The inmates, the lawyers, the judges, the doctors. Even the visitors sometimes. All of them can go to hell with me."

"How long have you been in here?"

"What that got to do with you, Sweet Cheeks?"

I waited for an answer anyway but never got one. Nail laid back on his cot again with his back against the wall facing me, then looked up at the night through the slender window. He looked lost in a memory deep inside himself. Under the fluorescent light, his color seemed to fade in and out of focus and sharpness. He looked luminous, then would fade into a blur of color and sound. I kept trying to blink him fixed, but it didn't come from me. I wasn't high anymore. I was craving badly. Nail staring me down only made me more nervous. I jumped up from the cot and began pacing again. I could feel his beady green eyes watching me intently.

"I got something you need right now." He said.

I stopped pacing at the door and looked at the guard's station. They were all laughing at the same cop, probably telling the same story as before. They looked more like they were watching the super bowl than cell dorm monitors. I wondered if they could see Nail and me from in there. I looked around for a surveillance camera inside the cell but didn't find one.

"What you think you got I could possibly want, man?" I finally said, turning back to him. At first, I didn't even notice the fat white four-inch line on the lap of his black jeans. Perhaps it was a loose thread or a rip in his slacks. A scrape of dust or a splash of oat smear from the breakfast he didn't eat. Before I could speak again, I recognized the line was a joint. An obese joint. If it were just tobacco, I wouldn't have been interested. And somehow, Nail knew that. The enticing way he looked at me told me he did have something I needed badly. And I would have it at any cost. At the moment, I didn't care what was mixed in the white paper. My hunger kicked in.

"Don't trust." Shut the fuck up, old man!

The dinner call and the open cell door saved me from further talk. I nearly fell through the entranceway.

"Think it over, Sweet Cheeks." Nail said. "I'm here all night." He howled like a warlock.

"You're not coming to eat?"

His laugh came to a sudden halt. He said, "I ain't hungry for that shit they servin' up. Remember what I taught you."

"Shovel it in," I remember telling myself quietly as I droned to my regular seat at the now-inmate full table. A stiff, nearly molded bun filled with chard minced meat greeted me when I sat down. This time, a carton of apple cider sat beside my plate of burned coal sandwiches. There weren't even condiments to drown out the taste of what looked like fried mud. Vomiting my meals had me hungry all over again, but I feared what the hard meat would do to my digestive system if I took a bite. I stared down at my plate, then picked up the burger and nearly broke a tooth biting into it. I expected my stomach to growl. I took that as a sign I was right to refrain when it didn't.

I was hungry for something more substantial, more potent in the bloodstream. Something that would make me forget for a time. And my Aryan brother had access to what I really craved.

"Don't trust, " hissed behind my thoughts.

I knew I should have listened, but what was the difference between the two lunatics? As if either of them were my ally. Whom could I gain from? The thought of getting caught didn't even cross my mind. If Nail had a way of getting it in here, he had some trick to smoke it without getting caught. I was banking on that.

I did think about my promise to Sara. And where was she? I'd heard nothing from her since that morning. I was still in the jailhouse. I deserved to get as high as I could. If only to forget.

Nail came to the entrance of our cell and leaned against the door frame, staring at me hard enough to burn a hole straight through my forehead. He was still bare-chested, wearing a playfully evil grin on his face. He taped his leg with his left hand like he was calling his dog inside. Between two fingers was the joint, slightly disclosed for only my eyes to see. Teasing me.

I quickly looked to the guard station. They seemed not to notice Nail or mind that he was there in the doorway, shirtless, barefoot, and carrying drugs. One guard stared directly into our cell. He didn't even flinch at Nail's parade.

I glanced at the faces of the other inmates. Indeed, someone else in this mob was as hungry for the high as me. But none of them noticed or paid any mind to Nail at our cell door entrance.

I looked for the old man and did not find him at the table. The cell door beside mine was open, but there was no sign of anyone moving around.

Had he been released?

No matter how I watched the others fill their cheeks with the dry, day-old bread and blackened meat, I couldn't eat the meal. No one looked to be enjoying any part of the meal. But they looked hungry enough to eat whatever was placed before them. I could tell by the stubble on their faces that most of these men had been there for days—some of them weeks. Perhaps they had no one to vouch for them or come up with bail money. Those men would probably never see outside a jailhouse for many years to come. I had no way of knowing the men I presently shared company with. They could be dealers, robbers, or even killers, and I was sitting at the table with them, breaking bread. The men all looked harmless enough. Ordinary men who had perhaps stumbled into some shit they had to fight to escape. It didn't matter the nationality or creed they lived by; we were all accused of something. Something got us locked away from society and those who tried to care for us.

I got up from the table, threw my uneaten dinner into the trash, and returned to my cell. Nail left the doorway and lay on his cot, looking like a corpse on an autopsy bed—the joint lay in the center of his chest between his firm pectorals, still as a whisper. As I moved to my bed, I tried not to let the wand of 'get high' entice me. His entire silhouette sharped in my eyes. His features showed more color now that the cell was void of natural light. He seemed even to glow, lying motionless with his eyes closed. I could have snatched the joint off his chest. It tempted me, too. But I couldn't. My temptation was to lunge on top of him. Hold him down and kiss and bite all over his bare chest until it was red and throbbing. I felt beads of sweat bubble at the top of my bald head and trickle down into my black face. I smelled my lust, and it enticed and shamed me.

"You like boys, don't you, Sweet Cheeks?" He questioned. His eyes were still closed. "That fight you had was with your boyfriend, ain't I right?"

I felt bold enough to tell the truth for once. I said, "I go with men. I don't rape kids—"

"I didn't say you did. You feelin' guilty about something?" He opened his eyes and caught me staring down at him, standing in the space between our beds. He smiled his wickedest smile. It was like he wanted me to try something with him. Perhaps he could floor my ego with his rejections while he continued teasing the desire out of me. I sat down on my iron bunk and eventually laid out to keep from staring at him. "I can smell a faggot like a burned match in a musky room."

"I don't want any trouble from you."

"I know what you want." He said. He faced me, propping himself up on his right elbow with his head in his hand. He let the joint slide off his white chest into his left hand. "I don't like your kind, is all." His voice was raspy and low. "Just thought you ought to know that." He put the joint in a pocket on the left thigh of his cargo pants and patted it down like it was a precious jewel.

The drug was in the room with us.

There was still the chance he'd share it with me if I played my hand right. Name-calling was nothing I hadn't heard a million times before – walking home from school or choir practice or to a voice lesson with mom in her classroom. Folks are always trying to hold someone down. Especially when you're trying to do right, all they were really doing was covering up their own lies, judging me.

Hate words became like rubber balls to a cement wall to me, bouncing away on contact, mainly when one had something I wanted.

I exited the cot and stepped closer to the toilet/sink to take a leak. I unzipped and pulled out and instantly felt the release of urine from my bladder. I didn't realize how long I'd been holding my water. I suppose I was actually nervous about showing myself to a strange and sick white man. But I couldn't hold it any longer. I wondered why my cellmate had suddenly turned on me. Before dinner, I couldn't get him out of my ears, and now the cold shoulder. I wasn't scared of him. His anger intrigued me.

I shook off, put myself back in my pants, and zipped up. I could feel Nail watching my every move the way Jamie would whenever we stayed together in the hotel room by the theatre. My bed had a bee-line view of the toilet when the door was open. Jamie would be sprawled out after we'd made love. I'd go piss, leaving the door open. Upside down at the foot of the bed, he'd make catcalls; whistle comments about how fine my backside was, especially from an upside-down angle. When I pictured the image, then—at the cell toilet—I saw Nail's face where Jamie's should have been. And on Nail's chest was a swastika tattoo in solid black bars. The image sent an icy chill up my spine.

"Nice package, Sweet Cheeks." Nail said. I thought he would reach out and slap my ass hard—maybe more than once—the way he laughed after he said it. I had to ignore him. Let him have his power play. It would only get me closer to what I really wanted.

I flushed the toilet and stood at the window, looking out into the night. Another day had passed, and I would spend a second night in a jail cell, away from my real life. An understudy would step into my shoes and play a role meant for my voice. Without thinking or caring about what was happening around me, I tried to hum some bars of the opera's overture. It was always how I'd calm myself before any show. I could hear the music clearly in my head, but nothing came out of my throat. Not a whimper. Not even a plea. The overture played on in my head, and I could not catch up with it. It felt like someone had stolen my wallet or my house keys. Softly, I grabbed at my throat.

No!

I curled away from the window to lie again on the stone-like bed.

Rehearsal was underway, and they would not hear my voice tonight. Miles, my spiteful understudy, would screech through the arias and tempt Danial into canceling the opening until my release. It was my voice they wanted in that role. My 'flawless tenor,' as some noted in several write-ups of previous performances of mine with Sara. The young, gifted, black vocalist was born to the underground musical legends. But I couldn't escape the rage I'd inherited. Being a remarkable vocalist and talented musician had nothing to do with being broken inside and unwilling to fix the cracks.

I wet my lips with my tongue. My eyes bulged against the fluorescent light as they stared into the sun. I turned away to check on my cellmate. He'd been reticent. I found him sitting on his cot, his broad back delicately touching the wall behind him. That flaming red hair danced like a campfire atop his head. He stared at me as if he could see the hot emotion inside me. Then he put on a charming grin that was bordering on seduction. He released a haunting snare that began in my head before it came from his face. I turned my head, embarrassed. I'm not sure what for, though.

"How'd you smuggle drugs in here?" I had to ask.

"I got your attention, huh?"

"Why haven't you smoked it?"

"Maybe I was waitin' on you, Sweet Cheeks."

"How'd you know I was coming?"

"Fireflies. Rats. Roaches." He said. "They come and go as they please and are full of information if you're inclined to listen."

"You sound crazy."

"Maybe I am. Or maybe you are." He said. He pulled his body to the edge of the bed and put his feet down. The touch made no sound when both boots hit the cement floor. I thought they should. "It's hot as Hades in this fuckin place. County ought ta invest in some air in these holding tanks. A convict could burn up in this trap!" He unbuttoned his pants. I tried to look away but glimpsed his tight white briefs hugging his firm pale ass and thick thighs. I turned to face the wall while he folded his pants and lay them on the cot. Where had his T-shirt gone? I hadn't seen it on the bed where he threw it in the corner when he took it off. He paced the cell. But I couldn't hear his feet touch the floor. He seemed to hover past me with each turn. I felt him glaring down at me like an obsessed warden. He started talking out loud, like he wanted the guards to hear him rant. No matter how badly I wanted to, I wouldn't turn away from the wall to face him. I was afraid of what would come after. "What kinda torture chamber is the joint, anyway?" He stopped at the toilet/sink. His eyes, scoping the back of my neck, filled me with a heat that grew inside me. "You ain't hot?" He asked. His voice was almost concerned. I turned to him to stop the heat from rising, but I wouldn't let our eyes meet. I stared at the stone floor. I had my hands between my legs like I was trying to keep them warm. It was the only way for me to hide their shaking. "Rats got your tongue?" He asked.

"I'm alright."

"You look cold."

"I'm fine."

"You're hungry."

I looked up at him, and his face morphed in and out of shape again. It could have been the dim light in the cell and night falling. It could have been my imagination. But before my eyes, Nail's face became faces from my past. Faces I didn't care to remember. Men, I forced myself to forget. Before my mind could identify one, it was gone to another until Nail's face snapped back into its place.

I wasn't high anymore. I was craving. How was he able to do that? Or was it my imagination? The faces were from my past. I got up from the cot and walked to the cell door to observe the social distance. He was baiting me. And I was open to getting caught up.

The room had become humid. I took my shirt off and decided the undershirt was too much too. I took it off too. Nail watched me undress while he sat on the toilet/sink. When I pulled my t-shirt over my head and saw him on the shitter, I thought he was taking care of business. Then I noticed those tight whites still holding in that supple bottom, spread out on the toilet seat. We stared at one another for what seemed like an hour, not saying a word. I don't know what I was waiting for. I suppose I was looking for balance. To watch his every move for a quick change. Then, interrupt it before it can finish the cycle. To catch him in whatever he was trying to do to me.

Nail finally got up from the toilet to lie back on his cot. He moved like I wasn't in the cell with him, as if he were in another space and time at the exact moment. I felt alone, watching him curl up in his fetal position facing the white cell wall. He looked as innocent and helpless as a little boy in the stillness.

The fluorescent lights flickered quickly above my head as if upset at my moment of endearment toward my cellmate. The space felt suddenly smaller than usual, and the stench of my piss lingered long after I'd flushed. I felt dizzy and lightheaded from the flood of feelings and memories. I left the cell door to retire to my cot again. Nothing would come of the night—all my hard work in ruin over a street fight with a boy I liked.

Another hour passed, with the two of us not speaking. I was drifting in and out of consciousness, repeating nightmares of the fight the night before. When I'd wake, from the moment I slammed Jamie's head to the ground, I'd drift off again to catch him and Steven making out more demanding than in the dream before. They would look at me and laugh into each other's mouths, binding tongues with each tease, raging in passion. Jamie's neck, a choker of hickeys, flaunted at me with every turn of his head. Steven was lost in lust. I attacked. I lost myself, and I attacked. Raging in red anger. I awakened. I needed to cool down.

"You gonna share that with me or not?" I had to ask. Nail didn't move or say a word. "Whatever you want, I can get it for you when we get out of here," I said. "I have money."

"What good is that in lock-down, Sweet Cheeks?" He asked, motionless. "You can promise me the world. I share my shit with you, and you run off like the rat your kind tends to be. What you got for me right now?"

"What can I give you?" I said, sounding feeble to my own ears. "I need to get high, man. Help me out."

"What if the guards smell it?"

"We'd smoke it all by then."

"You ready for drug charges on top of assault? Maybe murder?"

"I didn't kill anybody."

"You don't know that yet. Do you, Sweet Cheeks?"

"How do you know anything about me? You're in here with me!"

"I told you where I get my information." He said. "The walls even talk to me. I been around them so long." He let out a wicked holler of a laugh. It seemed to shake the room or the room in my head. I rubbed my hands over my moist head repeatedly, trying to keep my cool.

"We won't get caught. You wouldn't let that happen."

He turned to me then and said, "You damn right I wouldn't." He sat up on the cot and faced me then. Our knees nearly touched, but I couldn't really feel his close to mine. The Ora of him was stronger in presence than his actual being. I knew I would get what I wanted if I did whatever he said. All sense fell away from me as I looked into his wild, ivy-green eyes. There was no safety there, only the danger I'd been seeking. I need only follow to receive. "I know what you can do for me," he said.

"Tell me."

"Be my boy." He hissed.

The weight of his request didn't sink in at first. I thought about the camaraderie of brotherly love among black men in urban environments: homeboys and street corner thugs selling drugs and gang banging. 'Yo, you my boy' type talk. It seemed harmless enough. My next thought was of the man making the request. The man wore a Confederate flag on his belt buckle. And what the word 'boy' might mean to someone like him.

He stared at me with hungry eyes, waiting for a response. That hunger resembled the hunger I felt for the drug in the side pocket of his black cargo pants. What would it hurt to humor him? No one could see or hear us in the cell. But would he try something out in the open at the meal table? Make me look like a fool in front of the other inmates, trying to make himself look powerful? But how could some racist slur do any real damage to me in the modern world? He was a white fool seeking power. I could play along to get what I needed. I rubbed my head again, feeling the moisture thicken.

"I'll be your boy," I said. "In this cell only." I clarified.

"That's my boy." He hissed through a short, gritted smile. It was as if he were grinding me down like a toothpick between his sharp white teeth. "We'll wait till light's out and the guards settle to have our fun." He lay out on the cot again. "You'll have to hold out till then, boy."

"And so will you," I said. I returned to the window, looking for a sign the guards were getting ready for lights out. There was no clock in the main room or the cell. Maybe it was some mind trick to make us forget how long we'd been in lockdown. My one day already felt like an eternity. And in came another night. Only this night promised better. I couldn't see how desperate I'd become. How dependent I'd fallen. Completely willing to ingest something rolled in cigarette paper, not understanding what was in it or where it came from. Those questions never crossed my mind. The thirst needed feeding, and the meal was in Nail's pocket. What did it matter where it came from?

The more my promise to Sara tried to break through my addiction, the less I heard it pleading. I'd block out the moment in my memory before the words could speak again. I didn't think about the show or rehearsal or my understudy or agent; Danial looking smug in his director's chair, talking to a stagehand while we belt our bleeding hearts out for his direction. All I thought about—in my cell—with my Aryan brother was a white stick of smoke in the left lower pocket of his black cargo pants.

O night comes. Come sweet, black night. I drool at the idea of the high to come. The proposal of mentally casting off these stark white-grey walls tingled my spine. I couldn't keep still. I paced the ten-by-ten cell for at least a mile.

My hunger was too shameful to sit and stew in while being watched by my victimizing cellmate. I behaved like I didn't feel his eyes on me, like an actor inside his fourth wall. I thought I heard him snigger at me once or twice as I passed his head to glance out the skinny window. There was a tiny urge to turn to him, fight the urge, and call our arrangement off. I'd see Sara's reflection in either window; remember how much I'd hurt her—remembered the promise I made before she left me in the visiting area. In one impasse, I saw her with Mya. They were smiling, with tears streaming down their faces.

I looked at Nail; he had unrolled the pants and let them sit on the edge of the bed like they had legs in them. The pocket where I saw him put the joint seemed to bulge like packs of joints were crammed down. I walked slowly from the door to the skinny window, pretending not to stare at the pant pocket. My heart raced, trying to stay calm when I wanted to burst. Nail watched me with a pleasured smile rising on his pale face. I hated the power he had over me. I wanted it all the same. My mile-long pace had worn me out. I sat down on my cot. My eyes never left that pocket.

WITH THE DEVIL IN THE PALE MOONLIGHT

Ж

"**L**ight's out!" The voice said over the loudspeaker before the cellblock lights flickered three times, then snapped into darkness. My sight shifted, adjusting to the darkness. A slight glow of yellow light opened the floor from the window to the cell door, and a silver-gray moonbeam drifted through the skinny window from the night sky. The floating dust between the lights looked like tiny falling stars. I could barely see Nail in the darkness opposite me. He was sitting on his cot with one knee pulled close to his chest. The other is open. His white briefs seemed to glow against the black. Then his whole body looked as if to glow in the dark.

I hadn't realized my head was leaking sweat until a drop rolled into my eye and stung me hard. I squinted, squealed, and wiped my brow as more beads rose from my pours. When I looked up again, I found Nail twisting the joint between his thumb and index finger. The strong musk of marijuana floated through my nose and instantly put me at ease. Perhaps that's all it was. To some dudes, weed was considered hard stuff. Maybe all I had to look forward to was a dreamy night without snacks for the munchies. I'd take it if that's all he had. But the other stuff–the harder stuff–didn't stink until it was on fire. There's the other problem. Fire. He couldn't have that. Damn!

"You ain't seen no guards makin' rounds out there, did you, boy?" He asked.

"No." My eyes fixed on the joint he fondled with his fingers. His hands were in the space between his legs. "How are we going to get that lit? And how will we keep the smoke contained?"

"You ask too many fuckin' questions, boy. You wanna get high with me or what?"

"I don't want to get caught—"

"Then I'll just save this for a braver man." He reached for his cargo pants.

"No!" I said. "Don't do that." We both were still with the light beam between us and the stardust falling. Then I said, "I trust you."

He chuckled. "Ain't no other way."

Nail rose from the iron cot, walked the short distance to the skinny window, and began pushing at the bottom of the pane until a four-inch square popped out. Instantly, I could smell the cool, fresh air pouring into the cell like a waterfall. That alone should have been enough to free my mind. He dug his other hand around the crotch of his briefs until he pulled out a red Bic lighter. He leaned in as close as he could to the opening in the window and put the flame in the joint. He inhaled long and deep as the joint's burning head smoked on the window's free side. He exhaled all the smoke through the opening, where it triumphantly floated into the night sky. Nail looked down at me and smiled.

"You ready for me, boy?" He asked.

"Yes." My voice was meek—defeated, shamed.

Relieved.

I got up from the cot, and Nail made room for me at the window. Never letting the head of the joint come inside. The smoked danced against the blue-black sky like ballerinas in Swan Lake. I reached for the joint as he made more room for me at the opening.

"You gotta keep it outside, or the guards 'ill smell that shit, for sure."

"How did you do this?"

"What you worried about it for, boy?" My questioning irritated him. "What's important now is gettin' rid of it. Smoke!"

I inhaled longer and harder than I thought he had and felt the intoxicant run through my body faster than a lightning bolt. Sensations traveled through me like they were racing on a superhighway with no speed limit to slow them down. Emotions filled my mind and heart with deep sadness and the ultimate joy that only a child discovering something new could relate to. I surfed through my dreams and memories like flipping channels on a TV. And I hadn't even exhaled well.

"Blow it out the window, boy!" Nail's twang cut through my high and returned me to the cell. I remembered the danger and blew the smoke into the opening without fail. I even kept the joint outside. But I could still feel the smoke curling around my chest like a small animal trying to find its way out. One hit rendered me delirious and giddy. I suddenly wanted to feel my lips in the chilled air outside the window.

Keeping the joint out, I moved my face closer to the opening. I could fit my nostrils and my wide mouth outside the open space. I inhaled from the joint again, taking in more of the mountain's crisp air. I felt heaven open inside my brain and a light bursting behind my eyes. Then, that light exposed a fire—a burning building. The building I was in was engulfed in flames. I saw myself in the window with smoke and flames flailing around me. I was pleading for my life.

The vision startled me backward into the cell. The joint fell from my fingers and landed in the pool of toilet water. Quickly, desperately, I scrambled to the toilet, trying to get to the joint before it was too late.

"What's going on in there?" I heard a voice say from behind me on the other side of the cell door. There was no way I was going to turn around. Nail just laid back on his cot like he had nothing to do with what was happening. A beam of white light flashed behind me, hunting for something in the room. "What are you doing up, inmate?"

"I had to go to the bathroom."

"Well. Piss quietly and get your black ass back on your cot." The voice said. "It's lights out!"

"Yes, sir Massa, sir–"

"What?"

"I mean–okay," I said. The light stopped darting around the walls. The room was still again. Even the opening in the skinny window was back in place.

How?

I looked into the toilet for the joint and found nothing but wet white paper. Then the toilet flushed the paper away from my examination. I had not touched the control. And Nail was still lying on the cot, calm and collected.

"Well, you fucked that one up." He said. "Better get yourself calm before the guards have reason to come in here and do a search. You don't want them to find out what you been up to, boy."

It angered me that he wasn't as upset about the joint as I was. "You could have saved it." I said. "Why didn't you save it?"

"What's gone is lost. You can't turn back time — and all that good shit. Best to keep moving forward till there's a fork in the road. Besides! You ain't high?"

At the mention, I felt it. Racing through my blood and I was flying with my back pressed against the iron cot. The heaven I experienced opened again, and I was flying this time. Like the weed smoke, I float out the small square in the skinny window. I moved with the night air. And I traveled back to a bright and beautiful day in my memory that I'll never forget.

Every boy loves his first ride. I mean, the very first. Before, there's the driver's license and all that comes with it. I'm talking about the peddle-to-the-ground ride. The ride that dares you to take that steep hill coming or going; or dip between those two cars and cut someone off at a quick pass; one-handing it while costing, eating an ice cream sandwich kind of ride. My first was a BMX Redline. I remember being envied by all the kids on our block, and in middle school the year my dad bought it for me. That bike seemed to dare me to do the most dangerous stunts riding home alone as a kid. I found the limits in my physical endurance on that bike and pushed through them to make myself think faster, move quickly, and test my strength after another exhausting day of school and music lessons. Sometimes, before heading home, I'd go through State Street Park and ridge through the wooded trails along the aqueduct to take the bike off-road and really dare myself to let loose.

The high brought me back to one of those days when I felt most free, gliding through the tall, green trees. Listening to nothing but nature calling out to itself as I pass through. No piano noise to show wind in the trees or an oboe to signify danger ahead. Just the music of nature pushing the leaves. The swish of my wheels turning in the muddy earth. The clang of my hard peddling.

I was on the grounds near my home growing up. Those backwoods were filled with paths that trained me in the ways of the tricky streets of the real world. I was a high school senior in my vision now. Riding the mature Racer, I bought after bagging my first gig just starting high school. All the boys my age were begging their parents for cars, but I stuck with my bike. It kept me physically fit, toned, and handsome; it saved me a lot of money on gas, riding it wherever I needed to be.

I'd come home the back way that day, through the woods and into the backyard that was open to the wooded area. Mom would nag Dad about putting up a fence. She got scared at night, thinking something was staring back at her in the darkness of those woods. Daddy said he liked the mystery the openness provided. Mama was letting her imagination get the best of her. He never put up that fence.

I'd ride through those woods to prove to myself that there was nothing in those woods for my mother to fear.

I entered the backyard through the tall brush to find a flat, well-manicured, plush green lawn, the way I remembered it always being through the summers when Dad was home more often. That day, he was away from us, on a trip to a studio in New Orleans, engineering an album for an up-and-coming blues band. The Songbird trio was on a well-needed break from some tour, and Mom loved having the family home for a change. Even though Dad was away that day, she expected him home soon; I remember.

I laid my bike down on the grass and fell right beside it. The ride home had worn me out, and I wanted to feel the cool grass tickle my back and neck. I didn't think anyone was home. During those years, Russel was away, flunking out of college and causing trouble all over the campus. He was undeclared between his sophomore and junior years, riding a 2.8 GPA. My parents took a mortgage on the house to pay his tuition. We struggled, but Mom wouldn't let us see it that way. She always wore a smile on her face. She had dinner on the table with plenty of faith to hold us together.

At the end of my spread arms, I played with the grass at the ends of my fingertips, softly curling the blades and pondering my mother's heroism. She was the rock that held us all in place, and I wondered where she got all the strength to do it. Daddy was a handful and moody whenever he was home. I'm sure she wondered if he was faithful when he was away on these trips. He'd make good money but come home with nothing, saying he had expenses while down there. Mama made do with what he brought home. I don't remember her ever complaining or bad-mouthing. She kept that smile on her face. I thought long and deeply about her smile, and the day's sun seemed to move closer to our backyard. The grass felt like fire beneath me and smelled like burning chemicals floating above my face. The odor made me cringe and curl up my face, trying to block it out. Then I heard giggling coming from the house.

I got up from the grass to find the lawn was starting to brown in spots, and the rich green fur was turning to a burning yellow tint. I heard the giggling again. Two voices. The woman's voice I recognized as my mother's, but the man's voice was familiar but had yet to register in my mind. It wasn't my father's hefty laughter like a trumpet. This man's voice was deeper, more secretive.

That awful smell came again at me as I arrived at the house's back door. I could see my mother's back, her head to the left as she took a hit from a glass pipe with a long stem to her mouth and a bubble end at her hand. The crystal inside ignited and glared an intense red that seemed like a cartoon. She pushed the smoke out of her mouth like a dragon. It filled the view of her. And that sent—that rubber and coal burning in oil- pushed into my nose and through my brain like I'd taken the hit. I nearly gagged.

Then, as the smoke cleared, another figure appeared in the window. His graying head nestled in my mother's bosom, passionately kissing her breast. I froze at the doorway when the unnamed man lifted his head from her chest, and I found the face of Mr. Grime, Sara's father, looking back at me.

I remember landing on the back-porch floor like a goose feather discarded. I remember being unable to breathe because I feared Grime had seen me, and they would both find me and feel the need to explain what they were doing. But they continued to laugh. I continued to listen, and the burned scent of the drug permeated the backyard. I remember hoping a neighbor wouldn't call the cops.

In my head, I heard an echoing chuckle fill the air of the heartbreaking scene. It was a godlike sound that seemed to mock my discovery. Then I felt someone holding me close to his bosom. A man. A man's chest.

I swear, I woke for a moment from my vision. Back in my cell, cradled against Nail's broad chest. My mouth sucked desperately on his peanut-hard, red nipple like a giant hungry baby. Nail's head is tilted back, his mouth dropped, eyes rolling in ecstasy. The glow of him was so bright the intensity blurred me out again.

All fury, pain, pleasure, passion, desire, hunger, and grief converged inside me throughout that night in the cell. He brought me more than I craved and some of what I didn't want to remember. I would pay a heavy price for a high like this. I was aware, as I sucked from his life source. I found sleep somewhere in the night. I don't remember any dream beyond the one about Mom. I don't remember leaving my hidden position on the back porch. Just the growing sounds of sex-filled laughter between my mother and Mr. Grime, the hovering smoke leaking out the back door, and that putrid scent of burning chemicals. That day couldn't get worse. It had to have been that same month; I gave up the ride. I started taking the bus and using the front door to enter the house. It was the day I learned that every one of us was imperfect. Not one of us is without a crutch. Some are better at hiding than others.

WAKING

Ж

Bursting open to the icy burn of the fluorescent light, my eyes squint tight, trying to fight its loud glare. My bones felt like bricks, and the muscles and fat around them felt like the cement holding the house of me together. I was stiff and tight. Unwilling to suffer the pain of a slight shift. Only my eyeballs rattled around the sockets, searching the cell.

Some force—an entity, is the only way I know to describe it—with immense power, had me strapped to the slab of iron beneath me. Any struggle against that power was useless and caused prickling pain within my limbs, like something trying to get in and out of me all at once. Then— with little resistance—I turned my head toward my nefarious cellmate's cot. It seemed as if the force wanted me to see what wasn't there. My cellmate was gone as he had never been there. No sign of him at all.

Maybe he poisoned me and got set free just before dawn.

The taste of the drug was ten times stronger in me that morning. My veins ached for a taste of 'get high' like an infant's scream for its mother's milk. My mouth was dry as old leaves in a hot summer. Whatever it was Nail gave me, I wanted much more of it. My body needed more of it.

A heaving, warm brush of breath grazed my exposed neck. I felt the heavy dead weight of a body hovering above me on the bed. I heard a growl in my ear. I feared what I'd find if I turned my head toward it. It would surely end my life. I shut my eyes tight instead and waited for the presence to leave me or do its bidding.

The jailhouse wake-up bell rang loud, and the cell door slid open, crashing into the shaft. It sucked all the tension in the room out of the entrance, releasing the force that lay over me. I got up from my cot with a hard gasp for air. My head hurt behind my eyes, and I was hungry for more than just food. My stomach muscles clenched.

A hit. A shot. Anything to take the edge off.

The white light from the main room fell into my cage, forming a beam straight to Nail's cot, and there he was. Curled up in a ball of his own, half-dressed in his cargo pants and boots. Still no sign of his T-shirt. His image was sharp, bold, and clear, as if my eyes were the fools to miss him before. I rubbed at them to be sure I was seeing right. He was still there when I took my hands away.

He must have read the desperation on my face. He says, "I might have some more of that shit for you later, boy. Go on and see if you can get some breakfast down. You look like shit."

I couldn't say anything. I got up from my cot and went to the toilet/sink to splash cold water over my face. I felt much worse than Nail described. I felt like I was lugging around an extra pound of bricks in both hands.

I snuck past Nail like I was afraid of waking him. He turned his back to me, and that's when I saw the swastika branded on his upper right shoulder. The puffy, deformed skin seemed to show the mark was caused by a hot iron. And not by his hand. I gasped rage and fear all at once.

"Go on and get your meal, boy. I ain't hungry this mornin'," he growled, turning over. I hurried into the main room, nearly tumbling into another inmate on his way to the breakfast table. He looked down at me hard, like he wanted to kill me for falling into him. He was dark-complected, with dread studs spread out around his head. He looked like a thug from a porno or a hustler in a rap video, minus the gold. I didn't need any more trouble. I dodged his glare and headed for the end of the table to my usual spot.

Breakfast was the same gray pasty oats with a dollop of yellow butter melting over the mound like a glaze. The meal was grayer than the day before. The same oats warmed over, maybe. An obvious way to show the city had better things to do with its money than feed its accused a decent meal during their stay. The county jailhouse chef was a whiz at making ends meet by stretching the rations.

The growling in my stomach caused a pounding in my head. The inside of my mouth felt like sandpaper. My tongue was coated with a chalky substance I couldn't wash away in the cell. Another day without a bath. I could smell my funky breath and was smelling my musky, dirty ass. The dried vomit on the bottom of my pants. All of us at the table looked unclean. Unkept. I wanted to stand up and scream, 'I don't belong here with you criminals!' But who'd care? They'd probably laugh in my face or scream those same words back at me in unison. Who was I fooling? I was no better a man than any of them at that table. Probably worse because I had people counting on me to deliver. And they wouldn't let something as small as this hold me back from my duty. I thought, for sure, I'd hear something from Sarah that day.

Thoughts swung back and forth like a pendulum while I shoveled the creamy oats into my mouth until the plastic spoon scrapped the bottom of the styrofoam bowl.

My name was on the marque. My voice was the main attraction that got tickets sold in advance. The public coming to the theatre was expecting to see me in the leading role. O'tello. Not another random white tenor all done up in blackface singing the role meant for a true descendent of the fictitious Moore himself. I had earned the title after years of recital tours and small roles in little opera houses all over the country. Just to get heard. I had arrived at this role. So, what if I had been labeled disagreeable? I was known as the big black man with the mighty voice. Some had written that I was born to play the part. The company wouldn't deny me that.

A greater hunger deep within me drowned my career sorrows into a murmur in the back of my mind. I craved the taste of the drug more than I could ever remember before. It dizzied up my thoughts and clouded my head with nothing else but Nail's words before I left the cell:

'I might have some more of that shit for you, boy.'

Robotically, I chucked my empty bowl in the trash and retreated to my cell. I think the old man was staring at me during the meal. I think he wanted my attention. I couldn't look at him. I made myself pretend he wasn't there. He was a reminder of the promise I'd broken to Sarah—to the opera company.

To myself...

EMERGENCY REHEARSAL

News of my arrest hit the press. One headline read: 'Black Opera singer in the Slammer pending previews.' I didn't make any front pages, thankfully. However, the story reached the Denver Morning News on the local channels. Fifteen Minutes of Fame is now a headline for the Denver public to laugh at over lattes and egg muffins in early morning traffic. The media questioned whether I'd make it to opening night. And if I did, what shape would I be in to perform one of the firmest operatic roles ever written for a tenor after spending several nights in lockdown? Much of my ugly past was still hidden behind the rouse Sara and I had cooked up over our marriage and daughter. There was still no mention of my tragic family past and the murder my father committed in Denver many years before.

After we married, Sara came up with the idea to take on her last name over mine. We both agreed that even the small success of *Songbird*—the jazz trio album our parents produced together—would draw attention to the name Master. Just mentioning that name would stir up stories from the past we had to keep hidden to protect our future. To protect Mya. We had come so far as Grime. It didn't surprise me that people didn't remember the other victim's name in that Denver hotel tragedy years before. We always forget the victim. And my father was well-known in the music industry beyond the trio. Gratefully, his legacy and the violent crime he'd committed against my mother died when Sara and I gained notoriety in the classical community.

My newsstand street corner scandal stirred ticket sales – to the company's benefit. Questions were raised as to the type of man I was. The arrest events were unclear in the stories I was told about. The articles didn't mention the alcohol and drugs involved or that the two men waging war in the streets that night were possibly lovers. Jamie's name didn't come up at all. The papers described him only as 'the victim' and mentioned how he was rushed to Denver General with no condition mentioned.

The Colorado Opera House refused to release a statement concerning my situation. Their only concern was Verdi's Otello opening on time, as expected—the underlying message: with or without Cameron Grime leading the cast. I couldn't fault them for that. The show must go on.

The rise in ticket sales elevated the pressure on Danial to direct a great show. Emergency rehearsals in the Denver Opera House Grand Hall were underway as I sat through my third night in the county jailhouse, awaiting arraignment. The rehearsals were a vehicle to acclimate Miles James into the leading role. My role.

As any good understudy would be, Miles James was ready to step into my shoes—In all honesty, the shoes of any fallen lead—with only a few rehearsals involving the entire cast. Miles' diction was less than superb, but he was an excellent tenor and a talented musician. Audiences in smaller opera houses wouldn't notice the flaws like a New York Metropolitan Opera House listener would. Or maybe they didn't care. They are proud to have some remanence of the classics in their hometown. If the singer sounds passionate enough, stays on key, and in time with the orchestra, there isn't much else to strive for. And Miles James had an outstanding reputation with the company and his Denver audience. They loved him. And they'd probably love him greater after saving our production, playing the role of a painted-face Moore.

That year, the company showed diversity and took a risk in hiring me to play the leading role. They wanted a more authentic production than those done before at other, more popular opera houses. When our agent, Faye, got word of diversity talks, she told them about Sara and me. How I'd been studying the role since the start of my career and how well I had grown into the part. My goal was to go down in history as the black man that dominates Verdi's extraordinary tenor role – in Denver's production and productions to come around the globe. And my diction is perfect. They trusted our agent. The company received charitable support from donors all over the world. This show would solidify my stay in the opera community. And there I was. Locked away in a holding cell.

I credit the choice to make Miles my understudy to my reputation as irresponsible and unruly. The company begged Miles to take on the position as a favor for them. They would reward him with a feature role in two of the following productions that year. The stage manager of our production, Carol Loftin, and I are good friends. She said Miles smugly asked when offered the understudy role: "I'm a white man. What happens if I have to go on in his stead?" He knew the answer. He just wanted to hear them say it out loud. "I want the darkest mask you can find. I want to really look the part." He ended as he accepted the responsibility. Carol told me she nearly got up and socked him in the jaw. Instead, she left the room.

The cast had been working tirelessly those days during my arrest, getting Miles accustomed to the elaborate set and the staging. I was told later that the cast had more trouble keeping up with Miles than he did with them. His performance was impeccable. He never missed an entrance or fumbled an exit. It was as if he had been working with the cast since the start of rehearsals.

And he had. During my rehearsal time, I'd spot Miles prowling around the room, taking notes while watching my every move. I never thought much about him then. He seemed overanxious. Indeed, he didn't know I'd have to allow him to do what so many white men had done for centuries. During the process, his shadowing compelled me to scream at him to get lost. Those frustrating days when my voice wasn't right after a night out smoking and boozing up with Jamie. I promised myself I wouldn't even allow him to rehearse the role. I couldn't keep that promise to myself, either.

In the wings, he stood, poised and ready to perform. Face entirely made up to look like a human tar pit. I was told later about these emergency rehearsals. Sara, Carol, and some of the other cast members filled me in on the details of these rehearsals.

Sarah's aria swooned over the cast members as they again listened, spellbound by her beautiful soprano. She hadn't been at her best after the fourth time working through the high-toned legato aria that would take the wind out of any great female singer. And Sara was one of the best. I've always wondered why she wasn't already a Prima Donna of an Italian opera house with all the famous roles tossed at her feet. Sara's voice was as dreamy as a goddess crying in the darkness. I always feared her association with me was holding her back from her true potential. Our marriage kept the conductors and musicians from making unwelcome moves on her. They feared my big blackness. And she never expressed a desire to be married to anyone else, especially in the industry. Still, they lusted after her secretly when I wasn't around.

When she wasn't on call for emergency rehearsal, Sara would shut herself up in her hotel room, only taking calls from Ben, our manny back in New York, to talk to our daughter. She and Ben had grown even closer while I was using. He was the only person we trusted with our family secrets. Ben would comfort her and Mya when I was away from home at the bars or a phony voice lesson with a college vocal student I'd made up. My absence brought the three of them closer. Sometimes, I would get barely a wave from any of them as I crept out the front door to run the streets with whomever—doing whatever to keep my thoughts distracted and inebriated.

While talking to Sara over the phone from New York— during these emergency rehearsals—Ben suggested she write her thoughts in letter form to me. He suggested it would be like talking to me without intrusion. She could lay it all out on the table to get a better look at the situation in its entirety. She could let me read it or burn the pages and continue the way things were. Sara wrote that letter. It was over twenty pages, dated through the nights of the emergency rehearsals leading up to previews. Our stage manager, Carol, who witnessed the events Sara mentioned in her letter to me, described a portion of that letter— verbatim—to me later. Carol did not know about the letter.

Yet her account of the situation was nearly identical to Sara's:

As you adoringly call it, my lovely soprano cracked on the high note, pitching an alarming tone that caused our enormous cast and diverse crew to cringe and squint in torture. Some of them even grabbed at their ears. Ever since my visit to see you at the jail, my voice has been too sharp and shrill at the top. Like it was when I was just a girl, studying with your mother. Back when we were just kids with big dreams and a safe place to dream about them. The exquisite lyric soprano your mother helped me develop sounded like a pig's squeal while giving birth.

Danial jumped from his seat. With an exasperated waving of his hands, he silenced the accompanist. My chin dropped to my chest, utterly defeated. How could he expect better than what he was getting and still have us ready for a show in a few days? I knew he would give me hell because he couldn't pin this dilemma on the source. I was so angry with you. Unabashedly enraged by your careless abandon. Your habits and secrets have ruined everything we've worked on for years. And there I was, forced to take the heat for you again. You can be so selfish, Cameron.

"Will you be all right for preview, Sara?" Danial said as he walked closer to me to ask this in private. The room was so quiet I doubt anyone hadn't heard him down the hall from the echoing cavern of the rehearsal room. His approach was tender and gentle. Nothing as he'd been throughout the rehearsal process. He was probably trying to make up for the constant drilling of scenes. Insisting we sing the show full voice two and three times a day.

Miles James received not a single director's note. The company violated several union requirements with the strenuous schedule. Forcing some of the cast to threaten to report the violations if they didn't get some break. Along with overtime pay, the company may be required to pay fines and production costs. If no one else will tell you, I will. You should know all of this. You should know the damage you've inspired.

"I'll be fine, Danial," I told him. "We will all be fine for previews if you allow us to get at least one good night's rest. You have been running us ragged like slaves. Miles can play–" I couldn't finish my train of thought with him. But I will tell you this. Though his voice will never come close to the God-given genius that is your talent, Miles is prepared, convincing, and sober, even in that offensive blackface. I think the audience will sympathize with his choice to play the role that way. He's good. I apologize for my bitter honesty. He is exceptionally good at his job.

The piercing glares from the other cast members helped me realize how loud I was speaking. Some looked away, pretending to be reading the music sheets or talking amongst themselves. I knew they were listening. They all had a hand in making the rumors or spreading them around. They tried masking their pity, but I saw it clearly. Then, there were the members that snickered in the silence. Most of them knew about you roaming the Gay scene and could see this day coming from the start of rehearsals. Some of the local singers in the show knew your friend Jamie, and they told me they warned you about him. Of course, they thought I did not know your sexual orientation.

Surviving a rancid past has turned you reckless. And those of us in the path of your self-destruction take a mighty blow trying to care for you. My love for you keeps my faith that one day, you'll return to the man I've always known you to be.

"All right, everyone! We are on break for dinner and possibly into the evening." *Danial called out to the cast.* "Carol will set up a message to let you know if we will resume later tonight or pick up again tomorrow early morning." *Miles stomped out of the rehearsal hall with a start. He knocked over a few set pieces on his exit. He was mumbling curses under his breath. I assumed he wanted to get a full day's use of his blackface.*

The rest of the cast and crew rushed out of the hall with a whoosh of relief. As you know, this time for a cast—when the show is nearly open—it is vital to get proper sleep during the day to work hard well into the night. Working double time is brutal and seems unfair to those who don't need it. And we have come to Danial very prepared. He needs the production at its finest. It will blossom over the run. Danial is no good with hiccups or mishaps. He is a perfectionist. He cares for those who do hard, focused work for him.

When the room cleared, Danial and I stood in the center of the mock-up stage, down the center from my Death bed and your grand throne. He took my hands in his. We looked as if we were about to have a scene.

Carol was at her state manager's table, being as ominous as possible. Diligently, she worked on crew notes, waiting for Danial to give his next instruction. She had left the room, mentally, just like everyone else for the two of us.

I pulled away from Dan to sit on my deathbed. I started pulling the pins from the goofy hairstyle they designed for Desdemona in the opera's final scenes. You know I hate to wear my hair up. I'd rather have it in a ponytail or the ratty mess stuffed under a baseball cap. I thank God that Benjamin is so good with Mya's hair.

"Leave it up for a moment, please." Danial pleaded as he came a little closer to the bed. He reminded me of the middle-aged father any daughter would ask for. "You're lovely in this role, Sara. You must know this." He said when he stopped his advance to look at me. I'd forgotten what it felt like to be admired by a man truly. I'm not sure that I knew the feeling before that moment. "You know what he is doing to your life is strangling all your potential. He will destroy what budding career you have coming."

"I wouldn't be in this role if he didn't request I play it. There were other sopranos in mind. No one here thought my voice could handle it."

"They are not in the rehearsal hall with us." He said. I noticed an unusually cunning softness in his voice that didn't really fit his usual character. "You'll be more than glorious in this production. The public will love you. And those talentless wishers will eat all their harsh gossip talk."

"Danial?" I hoped he could see the plea in my eyes. "I feel like something is looming over this production."

"My dearest, that's Macbeth with the curse." He said with a grin.

"No. I know that." I said, smiling back at him. It felt so typical for a moment. "What I mean is, from the start of rehearsals, our production seemed doomed to fail." I had to

confess. *"Simply existing—leading church choirs and doing small recitals to come home to our daughter was all we needed for such a long time. Getting washed up in this sea of stinking success—don't get me wrong, I'm overjoyed at this success. But at what cost? A black man singing opera as marvelously as he–"*

"Is extraordinary. Indeed." Danial added confidently. "He is more gifted in the art than most. This is true. It's equally extraordinary that he can carry on the way he does, and his gift never suffers for it. How is that even possible? I don't know."

"Cameron has always been a fool. God protects His fools no matter how arrogant they can be."

"What about you, Sara? Will you let him take you down in those flames with him?"

"He's my husband."

"Is that really true?" Danial had sat down on your throne. He looked like an infamous white slave trader fresh from the conquered African village. When I glanced at him, he didn't seem like himself. The shadow of his brow had darkened as if something had possessed him. It wasn't so much what he said next but how. He didn't sound like himself when he said, "Through any arrangement, a husband should conduct himself in an honorable fashion to protect his family. Your knight has fallen from his horse, my darling. Into some real deep, stinking shit." Those words bit at me, and I nearly screamed back at him.

He leaned against the high back of the throne, and he returned to himself. I looked at Carol to see if she had noticed the change. She looked up from her work. We made contact, but nothing was acknowledged in her eyes. Later, Carol told me she heard and felt a change in the room when Dan spoke.

"You and your daughter deserve better."

"He's not her father." I don't know why I told him that. Perhaps because it's the truth. We need more of the truth now.

"I've heard talk about the two of you. I try not to take any of it seriously."

"None of that talk good. I'm sure."

"I know your husband is a magnificently gifted and rare talent—addiction has crippled his spirit. I can see he is living in denial of his true self. Trying to live up to an image larger than his massive frame can withstand. He needs greater help than the company can provide. It's unfortunate what has happened."

"The company can bail him out of jail."

"He hasn't even seen a judge."

"They should do something. We have a legal team—"

"That deals with contracts, singers, musicians, and agents, Sara. What do they know about criminal law? Can you comprehend what the press will say if the company lends a hand in this sorted drama? Do you realize what will happen to our show if we are in any way affiliated with Cameron Grime's drunken, drug-induced rage? They'd have a hay day with us. The news of his arrest is already spreading across the state. Stories don't take long to grow.

Thankfully, the company could find two black tenors who would replace Miles. One of them is from Cecily."

"What? Why are we rehearsing Miles? Why can't we postpone the preview until they release Cameron? It would be the right thing to do."

"The company wants no affiliation with this incident. They made that abundantly clear. They're already in a fragile state financially. You both knew that when you took on the jobs. This show was set up to save their asses, too. A drunken, gay scandal is the last thing the Denver Opera House needs–"

"And yet, ticket sales have soared since the news of Cam's arrest. The classical music community knows his name, Danial. The company hired him because of this mounting reputation as opera's badass black boy–"

"For his talent, Sara." He got up from the throne and exited the hall. "Not for this."

"Where are you going?"

"Your agent is on a flight in tonight. She wants to talk. I figured I'd meet her at the airport to let her down on the way to the jailhouse to scold your husband. She will probably try to gain my support to free our black songbird." He shook his head and turned from me, heading to the door. He threw his following comment over his shoulder as he walked out. "I've secured your good name with a company that will create a sizable production of 'Bohme'—as Mimi."

"Mimi?"

"In the spring! You would be flawless. They will call you. Be ready, Sara." He briskly passed through the double doors of the rehearsal hall, forcing them both open. A waft of foul air suddenly permeated the hall when the double doors slammed shut behind him like the closing of those heavy doors at the jailhouse. The overhead lights flickered frantically several times before finally settling. That pulled Carol's attention away from her notes. She was in the room again.

She looked over at me on the bed. I must have looked like a frightened child to her because she looked back at me with consoled and forbearing in her eyes. "You can't face that darkness with Cam. You know that, Sara." She said.

"I'm afraid I have to, Carol." Tears streamed down my face. "I owe him that much. He's been so good to me and my daughter."

"While neglecting himself in the process. Those skeletons want out of that closet."

"I won't just give up on him."

"I'm gay, Sara. It took me a long time to accept my sexuality, live in the god-fearing world, and be proud of myself. I tried to hide from my truth, but no matter where I found myself there, I was—staring back at me. You must give up on the fight to force him to find himself. The darkness will consume you both. And imagine what that will do to your daughter's future."

And here I thought she wasn't listening to Dan and me.

I stepped away from Desdemona's deathbed to come out of the set of the final scene. My rehearsal bag was in an open folding chair in our faux audience area. I couldn't wait to get back to the hotel room for a hot bath and a long talk with Mya and Ben in New York before her bedtime. It had been days since I had to say goodnight to our little girl. My throat was strained, and my heart was heavy with thoughts of how you were holding up. I had to ask myself: What help am I to you when I—in a way—encourage you to live in fear of who you really are?

I heard that foreign voice again as I reached for my rehearsal bag. Only, it sounded as if it started in my head, then somehow escaped into the atmosphere of the large hall. The voice called my name. Clear as day. I looked at Carol to see if she heard the voice. She returned to her notes and didn't seem to hear a thing.

It came again in a rasped whisper, like a hot summer breeze hissing my name again in a tormenting cycle. I turned back to the stage area and walked back to the bed. I noticed I left the hairpins on the bedsheets. The stagehands get so testy when we leave things on the set. I went to pick up the pins, and a shivering cold hand ceased the back of my neck. It snatched me around to throw me on the bed. Someone with the force of a powerful man had pinned me to the bed and covered us under the sheets. He pinned me down by my neck and right arm with his bitter, cold, rough touch. It became impossible to breathe. I fight in silence under the sheets. I hoped Carol was looking at this because I could feel it happening to me, but no one was doing it. Panic alone nearly frightened me to death. Then a cold, firm face leaned into mine and hissed in my ear like a heavy fizzing mist, "Your boy is mine, Songbird." I had never been so full of fear in all my life, Cam. A southern twang in his voice made it sweet and too sour for any ear to tolerate. I cringed away from what I couldn't see. But he was there. And for a moment, I thought I could see him tangled in the sheets. I certainly felt the rage within him.

"No!" I could finally croak out.

I heard Carol's feet scamper across the floor toward me. "Sara!" She screamed.

At once, the weight of the entity released me. I was gasping for air when Carol snatched the sheets off me. I saw the ghostly movement of air push past Carol, nearly knocking her off her feet. She grabbed one post at the head of the bed to keep from falling. The double doors to the rehearsal hall burst open violently, then slammed closed so loud that it felt like a harsh thunderclap. I remember it poured down raining at that very moment when it had been a lovely day throughout the rehearsal time.

Carol sat by my side on the bed. We both stared at the entrance as if waiting for some new storm to blaze through it. I investigated Carol's baffled face and quickly buried myself in her arms. I sobbed in terror like a child who'd seen a ghost in her bed.

UNSUNG

Ж

Through the dark, the faint odor of a burning chemical grew more intense. I was a boy at first. Stepping through the unlit room, trying to find my way to the black couch, invisible to the naked eye in a space just as black. My late-night quiet place. Adult man/woman laughter mixed with seductive moans sailed through the air.

Russel was out. Secretly courting Sara by then. My father is gone again. This time working with an artist in California who desperately needed his advice. Mother and I were home. I thought she was sleeping. There were classes in the morning.

I remember that night. I thought I'd buried it. But dreams find their way into one's reality.

I made it to my late-night quiet place. I was a very young boy then. My back pressed tight against the soft back wall of the sofa. My feet and legs crossed beneath me. That awful stench saturating the atmosphere.

The light from the TV in the corner of the room snapped on by itself—a display of digital snowflakes played without the sound. The laughing moans from the back room snuck down the hall and into the living room. Loud enough to know how it was being made. I was fixed in the black chair, paralyzed by the groaning sounds. The woman's voice was my mother's, only she sounded nothing like her usual laugh. More wicked—maniacal, sinister, exaggerated. At first, the man's cries were unfamiliar to my young, simple ears. But then I knew who it was. He came with the stench. Lately, whenever he came around, and father was gone, there was that putrid odor. The aroma of nightmares. What Hell must smell like?

Snowflakes on the TV turned to the Flintstones, The Jetsons, Super Friends, and all the other cartoons of my childhood downtime on Saturday mornings. That spot on the black couch became my quiet place as I grew. A place where I sit undisturbed. But that night, I couldn't sleep or sneak out of the house to romp around New York City. I was dead broke and between gigs with nothing but couch time to hold me over.

The putrid smell elevated to where it seemed like the usual scent of our home. Between the laughter, I heard soft but spiteful whispers that made me think of the biting of hungry dogs. I remember trying to focus on the shows on TV, but the channels kept flipping around. It played reruns from my young adulthood: The Jeffersons, Good Times, Different Strokes, and Benson. All the theme songs began to meld together like a chaotic medley, confusing and disjointed. Seductive, baleful laughter tickled the surrounding night from the backroom we usually used for guests. I remember wondering what my father would say if he knew. Deep down, I knew there would be no thought. No words. Only violence. He loved our mother. I thought she loved him, too.

The whispering met with the sound of hard slapping flesh. The sounds turned into screeches of passionate rage. The words they used turned taboo, and they sang them like a sick sex song. She screamed, "Fuck me, White Devil," "You want this white man's dick?" he groaned, and "Give me that ass, nigger woman." Anger pricked me like an arrow through my chest. I nearly found the power to break them apart.

I cowardly snatched the remote from the night table instead. Trying to raise the volume on the tube to drown them out. The TV remained silent. Then turned the channels and suddenly stopped at the production of Otello at the Colorado Opera House. My production. I recognized it from the final design of the set we saw in the theatre just weeks before my arrest.

There was the final scene in Desdemona and Otello's chambers. Her death bed. His thrown, the only set pieces dressing the stage. A backdrop of an ancient skyline in old Venice. Desdemona was kneeling on the floor by the bed, singing her prayers. The volume on the TV finally came alive, and Sara's sweet voice killed the sex sounds coming from the backroom. For a moment, while I listened to her aria, there was calm in my spirit and peace in my body. Like an opera lover at his favorite production, viewing his favorite singer in his favorite role for the first time. She captivated my heart more in this dream than when we first met in my garage all those years ago. It filled me with pride how far she had come.

Then the moment came when Otello was about to enter her chambers, interrupting her prayers to put her to sleep for the last time. The screen showed where I was to enter, and there was only an empty, inactive space. Worst of all, there was no sound from the vault where I was to enter. Yet the orchestra played on as if nothing had changed. The scene went on as if I were there. Desdemona would sing to silence and act out the scene as if Otello were there. Yet there was no sign of me.

Finally, I—or a ghost of me—invisibly had my bride at the throat on the downstage edge of the bed. Sara's head dropped over the edge. Invisible hands strangled her as the audience cheered on the scene with awkward adoration.

I was a child again. Curled up in the sofa's corner. Secured between its back and the armrest. The chemical burning smell was still heavy in the air. I was weeping. The laughter had stopped. It was quiet now. I knew I was alone.

The television went black.

Back in my cell, I felt myself grow up from the boy and out of the dream. Back to the man. Back to my hard, cold, iron cot. I was half in a dream when I squinted my eyes open to find the four gray-white cement walls, ceiling, and floor holding freedom from me.

Nail was dead to the world, or at least pretending to be, to avoid talking. Nothing but the wait to look forward to. I lay back down on the iron slab and dozed off into another distorted dream of my freaky past I'd been fighting with myself for years to forget.

The daunting weight of loneliness fell over me while I drifted in and out of sleep. It felt like I was the only one in the cell. Yet, an entity watched over me from every corner of the room. It could see inside my thoughts and feed on them like milk or food. I remember waking feeling more drained than when I fell asleep. Even napping was useless in that hellhole.

Isolation finally gave way to night. Nail had slept through his day, barely stirring, with his back to me the entire time. He was curled in a ball like an egg at the edge of a countertop. We both may have slept through dinner because I don't remember leaving the cell again after lunch that day. Perhaps they forgot to feed us.

The world seemed non-existent through the stillness of the night. I not only felt my heart beating in my ears, but I could hear it beating as loud as the thud of a mighty drum. No matter how curious I got about looking at Nail, that force in the cell wouldn't let me turn my head to see him.

I tried to rise from the bed, but a heavy force in the shape of an enormous hand pinned me down. The unfamiliar bee buzzing I experienced in the cop car returned to haunt me, rising from one corner of the room. Hissing like a rattler, it felt as threatening as an overgrown demon viper. The chill over me should have shattered me into millions of little pieces.

Then, a growling murmur filled the cell. An astounding aroma of sour, sickening death permeated the tiny space. The murmur turned to a chant that sounded like it was being spoken backward and underneath the chant. I heard my cellmate's southern drawl intoning in response to the evil moan. "Your will." He rhythmically repeated.

The hairs on my arms rose to attention. Chills ran rampant through my veins. The overpowering evil in the room was closing inward on us. Nail was praying to something unnatural. But what was it doing to me?

Finally, I craned my neck against the force holding me back until I saw Nail kneeling on the floor at the cot's edge. He rocked forward and back while repeating "Your will" like a medium trapped in a seance. Then he whipped himself over his back with an open hand when he'd finish the phrase. He slapped at his back hard enough to create whelps that would rise fire red, only to fall away just as quickly. The swastika on his upper shoulder blazed a bloody red stain and leaked thick crimson liquid.

My back pressed hard against the iron cot assured me this was no dream. We were under some spiritual attack. I dared to open my mouth to call out. No sound would escape me. The vice grip of the cold, enormous hand had a finger around my throat so tight I struggled to grab air.

Nail chanted again, "Your will," from a broken position on the floor. His body jolted back as if snapped in half. His upside-down, pale pinkish face was facing mine. His hot breath blew in my face. It stank worse than the reek filling the cell. His chin pointed to the ceiling, face elongated. Eyes wretched open, revealing only the frosty opal sclera that leaked from the sockets, slow, like melting candle wax.

Out of the darkness above his upturned face came a monstrous black head with horns on either side and bulging red eyes that looked like a fire in a globe. Its mouth filled with sharp grey teeth that shone through a slight sneer on the demon's lips. It was smoky black, like something charred in a deadly fire. Some of him was still smoking.

My body went so still I thought I had died. Perhaps I imagined if I made my body perfectly quiet, it wouldn't see me, though it was staring me right in the face. I feared that if I prayed, it would hear me and burn me alive.

Then the beast shoved past Nail's distorted body, moving closer to my face. I could smell the burning flesh of its slow cremation. I shut my eyes as tight as I could. The heat of it seared my face like a hot flatiron.

"We tethered his soul to us." It hissed. "Take him!" I felt those words simmer over my body like hot coals.

"Your will," Nail repeated back to it.

The moment I opened my eyes again, the heat and burning beast were gone. The enormous hand released me from the bunk. I leaped from my cot, falling to the floor. My body was soaked in sweat. I struggled to catch my breath. My heart raced, and I could hear it pounding hard and loud through the tiny room.

"More bad dreams, boy?" I heard Nail say from above me. "Pretty black boys like you are too weak for the cage. You sure you gonna make it to your bail hearing?" He laughed at me. Hard. It echoed the demonic chanting. Looking up at him, perched like the Cheshire cat from Alice in Wonderland on his cot, he was naked as the day he was born. His solid white body somehow glowed an intense gray shine in the cell's night. It seemed like he was made of dark light. Nothing human could look like that.

What does this mean?

"What are you?" I heard myself say as I stumbled to my feet, trying to crawl back into my iron bed. I felt hungover from all my years getting high, coming on me like a tsunami wave.

"You want to go higher, boy?" He asked. My ears perked at the suggestion. Instantly, I felt nothing but the hunger for the taste growing within until it filled me with thirst. Despite all I had witnessed, the mention of the 'get high' sparked my fancy.

"You got more?"

"I could take you out of this cell with what I got, boy." He told me. "What you got for me?"

"What do you want?" I knew it would come to this. I knew it somehow. "I'll give you whatever it is you want. Take it!"

"Even your soul, little black boy? The darkness wants your soul, and he'll take you higher than any tree you could climb. Salvation is in your sacrifice, boy."

"What the hell are you?"

"The master. I own your flesh. Lay with me, and I'll take you where you want to go."

"Lay with you? What..."

Whatever came over me that night locked me in its trance, leaving me powerless and functioning against my will. I stood over Nail's bunk and removed all my clothes as if I had been told to do so. My black skin seemed to bleed into the black cell until I became like the air, and the man I once was, a strong man, the survivor, was reduced to a slave of addiction.

Nail, at his feet, stepped behind me and pushed me down to his bunk. I lay on my stomach, motionless.

"The drug," I muttered softly.

"It's coming, boy." He told me. "Face down!" He ordered.

I did as he demanded. I felt a cold mass hovering above my backside. A haunting chill fresh from the morgue refrigerator fell over me. It covered me in an icy sheet of man. I quivered uncontrollably as the icy burning entered me through my bottom. It was like a strong, thick, wide rod forced up my ass with no mercy. When I opened my mouth to scream, Nail's cold, large, pale, glowing hand shut my mouth. The cold weight moved over and inside me like a million electric eels. The very touch of the flesh felt like it was eating away at my back while it plunged deep into my bottom.

Inside my body, a fire ran through my veins as I squirmed fruitlessly, trying to break free. Whatever Nail had become, he had power over me. The shock of the violation sent me into a dizzying trance. My brain exploded into icy shards at the passionate pain that ravaged my body. The strokes came in splendid, outrageous, raging, victorious thrusts that felt like years of abating punishment.

"Blackness be yo' mas'sah now, boy. His will have done with you." Nail laughed hideously.

But he came through with the 'get high' he promised. His injection was like heroin or crack would feel. Only a million times more potent. In my drug-induced lethargy, I re-experienced bathhouse encounters I'd grown ashamed of. The street tricks I took to motels or shady alleyways, to suck-off or frottage in a dark corner. Men, I didn't bother to take names from or wanted to see again — let alone remember. I was as careful with them as my inhibitions and inexperience would allow me to be. A few of the anonymous strangers tried getting close, wanting to talk when the act spent or walk me to the train, but I'd turn on them. Make them feel lesser than I so that they would run away in the other direction in a hurry. They could have killed me in certain instances, but the encounter would always outweigh the risk. A few stolen minutes, vulnerable to another man. Letting him see my desire and use it at his will.

I sailed in and out of those memories like they were happening in real-time. I could feel every orgasm, every kiss, touch, stroke, and caress with the intensity of a brilliant, violent storm. Better than I had experienced initially. My body tingled and glittered in the seduction. Yet, each time one experience ended, there was a moment of loneliness heavier than a ten-story building on my shoulders. I'd glimpse a shot of Mya's smiling face, looking up at me like a little, bright-skinned version of my beautiful mother. And the guilt would crush me. Then, another seductive memory would swallow me whole. Pull me back into the arms of an anonymous lover in a seedy alleyway, half-naked, committing another intense lude sexual act. Even I was getting sick of the filth.

On the way down from the high, I paid the toll.

That night, I dreamed. There was a reaching firepit in a bottomless space that couldn't be earthly. My flesh lit from the embers at the center of the blazing inferno. Entwined in millions of serpents, binding me to a fatter,snake-like body that stretches out for miles without a head.

I was not there alone. With me were all the men from the holding cell meal table. Intertwined by snakes. We were bound to the larger serpent-type body that fed on us as we burned, and the binding serpents bit at the men. Some snakes stay and suck from a vein. The men did not respond to the frantic bites. The biting completely absorbed the men in whatever fantasy led them to this hell.

I was finally bitten. The pinprick was momentary and followed by the sweetest sensation of ecstasy. Like the other men, I threw my head back and relished in the hot flames, toasting my soul. We were taken. Captured by our own persuasions. The anger that lived in all of us consumed our lives. All of us were locked to the vice it provided to distract us from the real problem we all needed to face.

Ourselves.

My consciousness was in two places. My body on the iron cot quivered violently beneath the cold block of my cellmate's hold over me. But my soul was burning in the unified flames of my prison dream. The intensity of the fire was just as palpable as the passion I felt in my fantasies.

I investigated the burning chasm, stretched long with snakes and fire feeding on an army of men. I found the Old Man, where he would be if we were at the jailhouse meal table.

He was unbound. Unbothered by the devil's flames. His white hair decorated his face and head like a halo of boundless victory. His black skin was smooth, like an ancient onyx stone. He stared at me with shame-filled, deep brown eyes. I only wanted to be devoured by the flames. His glare reminded me of Sara, Mya, mother, brother... father.

My father.

Finally, I remembered where I'd seen this old man before my arrest. He looked just like my father. Only older.

The age he would be now if he hadn't killed himself all those years ago. The tears that filled my spirit leaped from my eyes.

"Father?"

I woke in my cell with my body covered in cockroaches, other insects, and, I think, a few mice. They were eating away at my skin. I jumped from my cot, frantically brushing them from my bare skin, when it all disappeared.

My naked black body was sweat-soaked in the center of the cell, frantically looking around the room for whatever sense I had left. The cold stone floor against the soles of my feet assured me. Day breaking through the thin window let me know another morning had come. I was thankful for it. My bowels clenched, and I had to get to the toilet quickly before I shit all over the floor.

What came out of me was quick, wet, and smelled like a final fart at the end of life. It burned as it released through my rectum into the commode. I was terribly sick for at least five minutes on that toilet. Then, the cool dampness of my sweat calmed me as it ran down my bald head and round face into my broad black back. It reminded me of being baptized as a young man. Cleansed.

The cell was even warmer with life that morning.

I got up from the toilet when I felt I had dispelled all my gut could offer. I didn't want to see what fell out of me and into the bowl. I was afraid of what I'd find there. I flushed with my back to the commode. I gathered my clothes as quickly as possible from around the room, remembering how they were discarded. I put them back on. Sat down on the iron cot and waited. I was waiting for Nail to materialize on the bed. Curled in his ball, pretending to be sleeping. He couldn't be honest after what I'd witnessed last night. The real problem was whether I was dealing with hallucinations or real demons.

I believe in God, our Father in heaven, regardless of my lifestyle or no affiliation with any church. I am a believer. Religion was work for me. It was work that got me to church on Sunday. Why wouldn't the devil want to drag me to hell? Or had he done just that there in my private hell?

The hunger for his drug—for Nail—had grown more powerful than I'd initially felt. And I could feel his presence in the cell with me. Hovering. There was a haunting scent of him lingering in the atmosphere. But still, no visual signs he was in the room.

The rugged metal cell door charged open, followed by the loud buzz that signaled mealtime. I was glad my business on the toilet was done as the men walked by my cell, looking in to check for me. They filed out of their cells like zombies. Some faces I remembered from my nightmare in the firing pit. Those upturned faces in burning ecstasy now crunch in balls tight as fists. They found me in my tiny prison. A slight look of contempt flushed their faces. A sneered smile underneath their eyes. Had they seen me in the dream?

Was it a dream?

A burst of sharp pain shot through me, beginning in my backside, then up my spine as I stepped toward the cell door. It was a reminder. Undeniable proof that something took place. That something happened. To me!

I was sorer than yesterday morning or the two days before when they dragged my black ass into that jailhouse. I reached the table and sat before another bowl of butter-glazed gray matter. I was tired of the same meal warmed over another morning. I was sick of the same white walls, clicking chains, slamming doors, and the bitter faces looking back at me. Those eyes were full of hostility, hate, and confusion. I needed out of there. What was happening outside? Another morning–my third–and my future was still uncertain. This had to end.

I didn't notice that I stared into another inmate's face while he ate. He sat across the table, three seats down to my left. He was a large, burly, dark-skinned black man with a shaved head and a fat, crooked nose. He clawed his spoon overhand and shoveled the oats into his big face. I hadn't seen him before that day. Not that I would have remembered as selfish and bitter as I had been. By the third day in lockdown, all the faces blended into one sorry choir of moaning oppression.

I was thinking about Jamie and me on a date before things went haywire and the drugging and drinking got out of control. We walked on the gravel path around Cheesman Park under the tree line. The sun was out in a clear blue sky, and the grass was greener than I'd ever seen grass before. All the park colors seemed to pop out at us under the sunbeams. I remember looking at Jamie as we strolled down the lane. His long, broad body sauntered beside me like a white tiger. He caught my eye and reached for my hand, and I shied from him, looking around the park to be sure no one had seen us. He howled a hard, sour laughter that would surely draw attention to his flailing. I hated when he acted faggoty, like a city queen. And he knew that. He quickened his steps to get ahead of me. I trailed after him but refused to apologize. He never wanted to understand our arrangement.

He never knew the whole truth until the night of the fight. I never spoke about it.

"What the fuck is you lookin' at, faggot?" a growled voice invaded my memory. "You Gay, niggah?" It was the crooked-nose black man. He'd finally looked up from his bowl and found me staring at him. Whatever he saw in my face enraged him. "You want some of me, faggot?" He yelled across the table, getting up to his feet. He grew the size of a mountain, square and diesel-like a Mack truck. He walked toward me. I got up from my stool.

The both of us burning for the confrontation—longing for some human contact. I needed that angered connection more than the breakfast they served. I saw the rage on his face that I felt in my heart. The urge to swing, punch, and jab until spent. Some other men stood up, hounding us to make a brutal scene.

"Kick his black ass!" One man shouted.

"I heard that sissy crying out in the night." Said another. Was he talking about me?

"Give him something real to cry about!"

"Show him what it's like in county lockdown. Yeah!"

The crooked-nose man came to where I stood and faced me with his arms arched at his sides, ready to take the first punch. But he hesitated. I was ready to fight. I wanted to. Without knowing, I had balled my fist tight and arched my arms slowly. Waiting.

The main door to the holding cell whooshed open as the guards swooped in to surround the men at the table. There may have been ten men to the twenty inmates in lockdown, but the cops had weapons. Lots of them. Tazers, bully clubs, shields, and even a few guns. What kind of battle would this be? The officers seemed willing to take us by force should it come to that. But the fire in the eyes of each inmate burned hot like my own. We wanted the fight.

"Get your asses back in your fuckin' cells. Right now! Girls!" The voice blared over the loudspeaker like a god of thunder. For a long moment, no one moved. Suspended around the table, waiting to see who would make the bold move to set this scene a blaze. Every man in that cell wanted to lay violent hands on someone else. Anyone else? The tension was thicker than fog coming off a river. It was all we had in common.

"Your cells! Now! BITCHES!" The booming voice came again over the loudspeaker. I remember the lights flickering just before the guard screamed again.

Looking into the smoked eyes of my adversary, I realized that my fight wasn't with him at all. It was myself I wanted to hurt. For all the wrong I had done to everyone who loved me. I was ashamed of myself then.

"I'm sorry," I said to the crooked-nose black man. My arms relaxed, and my fists released to open palms. "I was lost," I said.

"Fuck you, man." Came the answer from his black face. He turned from me and broke through the circle of inmates and guards to return to his cell. The other men broke away, disappointed at the outcome. The guards relaxed as the inmates did as they were told. They abandoned the empty bowls and empty stools at the table.

I stepped towards my cell before a hand slammed down on my shoulder. The owner twisted me around to face two guards with caps that covered their eyes, their faces blackened by the shadow cast by the brims of their hats.

"You've got visitors." One guard said.

SOMETHING WICKED HAPPENING

Ж

The judge will see me today?" I asked Faye. "What's today?"

"It's Sunday," Sara said, pacing the room.

"She's willing to make the exception under the circumstances and with all the media talk." An older, tall but thinner, light-skinned gentleman explained before he sat down at the table with Faye and me. He wore an awfully expensive gray suit and matching tie. He looked like the type of black man you wouldn't want to debate any issue of importance with. In his eyes, though, was the sensitivity of a gently stern grandfather.

"Media?" I looked at the three of them for answers. Faye wore a sorrowful smile. The older black man looked sorry for me. Sara wouldn't look at me at all. "This made it to the papers? Why?"

"The Opera House is an internationally accredited theatre, Cameron," Faye said. "Did you really think something like this would go unnoticed?"

"You didn't make the front page," Sara said over a shoulder. Still pacing and avoiding my eyes. I needed her to sit still.

"What are they saying? Did they mention anything about Jamie? Is he all right?"

"Jamie? Jamie!?" Sara turned on me. "What the hell, Cam–"

"Sara, please calm yourself. Sit down, sweetie." Said Faye.

"I don't want to sit down." She was biting at the cuticles on her right hand. I haven't seen her do that since she was a nervous little girl. She paced again. Faye turned back to me and took my shackled hands into her own. My wrists were bound and bolted on the table's surface. The older black man looked utterly unbothered by the show in front of him.

"Cameron," Faye said. "This is Walter Hamilton. He will represent you through the arraignment and trial—if it comes to that."

"Trial—" I said. "What in god's name—I got drunk. I had a fight in the street. It's hardly a matter for the courts." I looked to Sara to give me some word that the company had something to do with this. That they had stepped in and got me in front of a judge on a Sunday. She still wouldn't meet my stare.

I looked then to Faye, whose face had gone a pasty white. Diminishing the rose-red glare that naturally beamed in her round chubby face. She pulled her pudgy hands away from mine and clutched at her purse as if I'd turned into a bum on a New York City subway car. I nearly laughed at her.

Walter Hamilton was my only hope of getting any information out of the group. I glared at his stoic, brown-faced salesperson expression. Looking for answers that he probably did not know. But his face carried a mighty weight as if he couldn't be swayed. I trusted him. I was afraid to ask what came next. I am quiet.

Sara suddenly stopped pacing the room and looked directly at me. She was searching for something in my face, an answer of sorts. Then she squinched her upper lip into her nose. Then gently thrust the knuckles of her fists into her nostrils as if trying to filter a scent.

"Are you okay?" I asked her.

She turned away from me. Returned to her pacing track, looking more like Lady Macbeth than the desperate Desdemona clinging to love and life.

Faye ignored her. Walter Hamilton just stared at us like we were sideshow freaks.

"Walter is one of the attornies for the Colorado Opera House—"

"I'm mainly a consultant to the company, but Faye is a longtime friend, and she called me about your situation," Hamilton explained. "I thought I might lend a hand. I know the sitting judge well, and she welcomed the favor."

"So, you can get me out of here tonight?"

"Hold on, Cameron. It was hard enough arranging this meeting with you and the arraignment today." He said. "You can thank the press for making such a big stink about the incident. The judge is a huge fan of the company."

"Then I should be out by tonight," excitement overwhelmed me, "for rehearsal."

Faye said, "The company is worried for you, Cameron. And they do want to help, but they want you to agree to treatment."

"Treatment? For what?"

Both women simultaneously rolled their eyes and sighed in absolute frustration. Faye tried to mask her disappointment, looking down at the table between us. Shaking her head softly. Lifting her head to me again, there was a fake smile plastered there like a mannequin. Sara had no discretion, however. While pacing, she mumbled to herself. It sounded like the demon in the corner of my cell for a moment. Then she turned to me. The anger in her face exploded in her cheeks and forehead as she said, "Treatment for your addictions! For this lifestyle that is killing you and our careers. Treatment for this livelihood. Do you even understand how much damage you've caused?"

"Someone tell me how Jamie is doing." I pleaded. "Does anyone know how he is doing?"

"It's your own life you need to worry about now," Faye said.

"Actually, Faye," Hamilton finally chimed in again. "Cameron is right to inquire about the status of the victim he's suspected of violating."

"Oh, I hit him. I'm guilty of that." I said.

"Let the courts decide your guilt or innocence, Mr. Grime. Till then, you shouldn't talk to anyone but me about the incident. At least until we know more."

"So, we know nothing about Jamie?"

"What is that smell?" Sara asked from the corner of the room. She stopped pacing to stand there. Her eyes squinted hard at something in front of her. Her brow scrunched above them. She looked terrified. Her entire face looked pitched between a giant's index finger and his thumb. "It smells like rotting meat in here." She said. "Can none of you smell that?"

Faye and Hamilton stared at her, bewildered. I assumed they didn't smell the putrid odor.

"Sara, the last thing I need is for you to lose your head while our lead is behind bars. Talent, can we please save the dramatics for the stage? We need to get to opening night." Faye said. She was beet red now as if she were swelling. She fumbled through her purse to snatch a white napkin from it to dab her forehead and lightly sweating face.

"Everything is going to work out in our favor." I tried to assure her. "The company is considering letting me go on, then." I looked at Hamilton, but it was Faye who told me the news.

"They've considered letting you sing the final week of the run if you agree to treatment."

"Consider?" I asked.

"They've agreed to pay for your treatment here in Colorado," Hamilton said.

"Consider," I repeat.

"I can't afford these happenstances again, Cameron. I did the best I could. Pulled my best resources. You've burned too many bridges. We need a performer on that stage who will deliver the role like his life depends on it. I used to believe you were that man. But now your crutch has landed your name in the paper as a laughingstock. Not for the talent the world deserves to see."

"Faye. Don't talk like this is over. I may get out of here today. Isn't that right, Mr. Hamilton?" He gave no response. Just a stone face staring back at me. I went on. "I'll get a request for bail and the company..."

"The company wants nothing to do with this story," Sara said bitterly. The room went silent. I realized we had spilled the beans. They were trying not to tell me, but the company didn't have my back at all. I was shocked.

"I'll change my ways. I can do better."

"Do the treatment. Let them see you will work on this addiction." Faye said. "Maybe they'll give you those last shows to redeem yourself."

"I can't represent you without their consent, Cameron." Said, Hamilton. "You need to agree to this so that I can help you."

"This looks bad," I said, sinking my chin into my chest. "But I can turn it around. You need to get me out of here. I'm seeing things..." I said quietly. "I'm losing my mind in this place. Something wicked is happening to me in my cell..."

"Oh, my god." Sara chimed in. She sounded genuinely concerned, as if she knew more. Something she was ashamed to admit.

"I sound crazy. I know that. It feels crazier. Something is happening to me here. It's messing with my head."

"Could be detox," Faye said.

"Do you have a cellmate?" Hamilton asked. "I can try to have you moved if he's caused you any harm."

"You need to get me out of here, Mr. Hamilton," I said, a little sharper than I intended. He didn't seem to take offense. "I think I've been... violated." The words didn't sound right to my own ears. Hot, wet tears of embarrassment rolled down my cheeks uncontrollably. It happened to me. I still ached from the act.

It was Faye who got up from the table to pace the floor now. She seemed frantic from deep within, itching for release.

"We have to report this." She said. "They have to move you to a safer holding cell."

"I don't think my rapist is real, Faye," I said, in the purest of honesty.

"Dear lord, you are losing your mind." She said.

"When they put me in my cell that first night, there was no one in there with me. The next morning—after I visited with Sara — I got back to my cell and there he was. He had a joint–"

"For Christ's sake, Cameron. In the jailhouse!" Faye shrieked.

I continued my confession.

"We got high. I'm sorry, Sara. I know I made a promise to you. But when I didn't hear any more from you—I got weak. I needed something to take the edge off."

"Your cellmate had drugs on him? In lockdown?" Hamilton asked.

"Yes. Yes, he did. I wondered how, but I didn't ask. The cops didn't strip search me when I was booked. There was a soft search when I was handcuffed but—"

"Why do you think he's not real?" Sara's soft voice asked from the corner of the room.

"Because he's not there now. And he doesn't eat. He sleeps all day, and at night, he's working me over. And—there was a beast in the room."

"That's it," Faye said. "You are going batshit crazy–"

"Faye!" Sara screamed in my defense.

"Don't tell me you believe this bullshit. Sara, this is some drug-induced delusion he's cocked up to gain our sympathy. Look at him! I should have known better than to think he was going to straighten up without me around to kick him in his black ass. You're ridiculous, Cameron Grime. Ridiculous!"

I stood up, and I said: "No one in this room can think this is more insane than I do. No one! But an entity violated me–in my holding cell–. A demon, maybe. I'm under a lot of stress—yes—but this pain is real. Now, you tell that company to get me the hell out of that cell, and I'll sing that role like a black canary set free on a summer's morning. I will make you money, Faye! Just get me the hell out of here!" I viciously slammed my cuffed hands on the tabletop. I nearly lost my balance and fell onto the table, remembering then my feet were shackled too.

The door thrust open, nearly knocking into Faye. She jumped back from it just as my escorting officer bailed into the room. His left palm pressed against the butt of his weapon. "What's going on in here?" He looked at Hamilton. "Was I wrong to allow you to interview him without me present?" His question sounded more like a statement.

"My apologies, Officer Downs," my lawyer said. The familiarity in their exchange encouraged confidence in me toward him. He works fast. He had already gained an alliance with Denver law enforcement. The chance of getting out today grew within me—even if it was just a small step.

Officer Downs shot a hard and swift look my way. It insight an unspoken order I knew to obey. I was on my way down to my seat when he said, "What are you doing on your feet, inmate?" My butt was already in the chair.

Faye didn't waste a moment getting in Down's face. "Does he have a cellmate?" She asked, looking like a mother scolding her towering teenager.

"No, Ma'am." Downs said. "I put him away myself the night we hauled him in. I made sure he got a cell to himself because I knew who he was. Didn't want him to get in any trouble." Downs turned to me and said, "My wife is a huge fan of yours. I was trying to tell you that night—"

"I remember you," I said humbly. "Is there something I can sign for her?"

"I haven't told her you were in here." Downs said. "She doesn't follow the news. She says telling her about my day is all the news she can stand." Downs narrowed his fixed gaze before he went on. "She's a music teacher in Arvada. Her class has plans to catch that Otello production when it opens. She raves about how well you sing to anyone who'll listen. She was a fan of your father's trio, too, before all that happened years back. I didn't want to break her heart telling her what a drunken, drugged-out fool you turned out to be that night. She'd probably give up all hope in classical music." He said.

"She teaches music, huh?" I asked.

"Sure does. And she loves teaching the classics." He said. "Those kids were pretty excited about that show, too. I hope you make it out of here in time?"

"I'm going to try, Officer Downs." That was the truth. "Do you know what happened to the other guy in the fight? The man they took to the hospital?"

"Listen, I don't have spare time in my shift to dive into the details of your foolish drama." Downs said. "You were out of your mind, drunk, high, and raging like a bull. That guy could be dead with the way you were beating his head into the ground when we showed up. Good thing you got a nice enough lawyer and some support that will hopefully get you out of here in time for my wife and her class to see you perform." Downs paused in his lecture.

The odor Sara complained about earlier I could smell in the air now. I could smell it then, but it was faint. I even thought it was my own filthy ass. The stench grew stronger then. I wondered why the others didn't react to it. Sara's knuckles rose to her nose speedily.

"You've got five minutes before the judge is ready for you." Downs said after glancing at his wristwatch. "Use the time wisely."

"Instead of hunting ghosts," Faye said under her breath.

"I want to talk to Cameron alone for a moment," Sara said.

"I don't think so." Downs said immediately.

"Officer Downs, you know this man is not a threat," Hamilton said. "Your wife would vouch for him. This is his wife." He gestured to Sara, bringing her closer to the fold. "Let them have a moment. I'll be standing right outside the door."

Downs glared at me and said, "I'll be standing right next to him. Make it quick."

Sara waited until they were all out of the room before she looked at me. Her face met mine, and I saw her soft, square cheeks slightly sunken in. The brightness in her blue eyes seemed shattered in a million pieces after years of battle with my addiction, my deceptions. It had finally taken its toll. And I bear witness to the damage.

"I know I sound crazy. But I'm telling the truth." I said.

"I believe you." She simply said. "Something happened in rehearsal last night. Something wicked, just like you called it. I can't explain it now, but whatever it was, it came from here. It came after me. Don't let it—whatever this is—

destroy you, my friend. Its power is strong, but you don't have to go where you don't want to. Do you hear me?" I heard what she said, but I heard it in another voice from inside these walls. It was the old man. The old father's voice. She was speaking madness that made complete sense.

"When this is all over, we need to divorce."

"Sara, don't be ridiculous. We'll make it through this together."

"I don't want to. This is your fight. I can't be a part of the lie you keep telling yourself. It's killing me. We were never in love. Not in that special way. What's the point of pretending? The truth will make things better for us both. Especially for Mya."

What was there to debate? She was right. The demons were mine to face. I could no longer use Sara as my shield.

She got up from the table as my attorney opened the door to poke his head in and announce, "The Judge is ready for us."

Sara left the room as I followed her out with my eyes. I got up from my seat when I remembered they had shackled me to my abandonment. Officer Downs poked his head through the door and told me to wait for his men to come for me.

"Why can't I go with them?"

"Because you committed a crime, choir boy." He said. But It wasn't his voice. It was another familiar voice. Then he swiftly slammed another door in that wretched custodial. We were finally alone.

What I couldn't tell anyone while we met was that Nail was in the room with us. At first, I could only feel his presence hovering between us. There was a slight blink in the overhead light, and the unmistakable heat spike from time to time. It was when Sara mentioned the unpleasant odor the second time it got in her nose I saw him standing in front of the corner. She walked right through him when she came to the table to sit down. He watched Faye pacing the room with his arms crossing his chest, leaning against the back wall like he was on a street corner, looking for his next prey. I thought I was hallucinating until Officer Downs assured us I had no cellmate when they booked me in there on that fight night.

Nail didn't see me watching him. His form was translucent, like a thickening of air around a body. He didn't look at me at all during the meeting. He was feeding on and filing their rage whenever they would release it on me. His presence fueled their little madness.

He was in the room with me then while I was alone. I felt him there. But I couldn't see him anymore. My shadow began to dart around the floor and the four walls like it were dancing at me, mocking my shackled wrists and ankles with its freedom to move about the stale white walls. I followed it with my eyes, amazed at the dancing taunt as it stretched along the ceiling, growing into a massive, menacing black cloud above my head.

The overhead lights flickered wildly like strobes. A panic rose in me with a wild urge to break the chains and destroy the room. Inside, my gut burning began the way it had when I caught Jamie kissing Steven outside the Winbro Apartment building, the heat I felt as a young man curled up in my secret place on the black couch, smelling crack cocaine in the air and listening to sex coming from the back room, the heat of trying too hard to hide my true self from myself and the world. I sweated profusely. The shadow performed acts of violence in my head through its dance. It threw the chairs and banged on the table like an ape thrashes the air in a wild dance.

I heard Nail tell me, "We own you, boy." And laughed viciously.

When the door to the room opened, I jumped from my seat again. The black officer entered the room with a start. Only he reached for his gun.

"I'm good!" I alerted him.

He relaxed when he saw I was shackled to the table and couldn't possibly escape.

Another long walk down another long white corridor led to a wooden bench across from a door that read 'Court Room A' on a gold plaque in the center. I sat there staring at the sign while the guard stood above me as if I were his watchdog. We weren't there long before another guard opened the courtroom door to signal me inside.

SUNDAY HEARING

Ж

I walked into a portion of the courtroom boxed in the main room by a wall of thick, floor-to-ceiling, bulletproof glass. Inside the space was another wooden bench I was told to sit on next to a white man who looked just as worn and weary as I felt. There were sets of tiny round holes about five feet from the floor to the center of the glass walls. The tiny space was stuffy, stale, and claustrophobic—a perfect area to do his bidding. The thickness cloaked us. I felt like a wild animal, caged.

I did not recognize the white man I sat beside on the bench. He didn't come from my ward. He wore a silky black goatee around his middle-aged face. He was thin but muscle-bound. His arms and legs were lined with lean, powerful biceps, abs, thighs, and calves. The fear didn't show as much on his face as in his body. Rapidly bouncing the leg closest to me and rubbing his thigh with cuffed hands. He was sweating, too. I wondered what made him so important that he got to see the judge on a Sunday, too.

Both of us were ungroomed. The strong musk growing in the small chamber reeked sour sweat and worry. He didn't bother to look my way. I doubt he even realized I was there.

He had been so caught up in his trauma. No one looked at me when they hauled me into the room.

Proceedings seemed in place. A tall, thin, graying lawyer pleaded his case to the judge from the prosecution table. His voice was too loud for the cramped chambers. The court was smaller than I expected it would be. The gallows' brown wooden benches with the small jury box tightly crammed into the gallery. The furnishings seemed too large for the area, making the room look like a staged abstract courtroom drama set.

The bar was half filled with on-lookers scattered about the seats. Most seemed to be reporters with cameras around their necks, scribbling on small rectangular notepads. They fidget around the courtroom impatiently, like they were waiting on a train.

The white man sitting next to me was called to stand before a set of tiny holes in the glass wall. He sobbed before getting up from his seat. The weight of his tears forced his body to shiver. I thought he was going to explode the way he was shaking.

"Step forward, Mr. Charles." The judge's voice reverberated through the room as she pushed away a curl of wild red locks from the view of her green eyes behind black, horn-rimmed glasses. She pressed her glasses onto her face and glanced at the paperwork. She looked slightly over fifty—still, youthful prance searching the room and the pages at the bench. "You are being charged with attempted murder in the second degree. How do you plead, Mr. Charles?"

He could not respond through the fit he was under.

"Mr. Charles, is something the mat—Where is this man's representation?" She looked around the galley for the answer to her inquiry. She was visibly agitated when there was no response. The thin, graying lawyer stood up suddenly at the large defense table to address the court.

"My client has suffered a great deal of duress during his stay at the sheriff's jail, your honor."

"And what does that have to do with your client's plea in my courtroom, counselor?"

"Mr. Charles would plead 'not guilty' to the charges presented by the prosecution. He requests release on his recognizance—"

"On a murder charge, your honor?" Another attorney— tall, athletic build, middle-aged— stood at the prosecution table, his chin up and chest out as if he'd already won the case.

"I would have to agree with your sentiment, prosecutor Thorn. What is your recommendation?"

"Your honor, with all due respect, Mr. Charles is being tormented in his cell while in the police's custody. I don't think he's safe here."

"We can move him to another cell if his cellmate is harassing him."

"He doesn't have a cellmate, your honor." The defense attorney said.

I looked up from my shoes at Mr. Charles. His trimmers heightened. The back of his shirt was wet with sweat. Mr. Charles looked like a tough guy who didn't scare easily.

Whatever was tormenting him in that jailhouse was something he couldn't get control over or even defend himself against.

I could relate to his fear. I wanted to stand up and testify in his defense.

Mr. Charles spoke instead. "It's trying to kill all of us in here. Everybody's just scared to say what it is. They don't want to talk about it!"

"We'll have order, in my courtroom, Mr. Charles. You speak when spoken to and not before then."

Mr. Charles suddenly turned to me and screamed, "You know what I'm talking about! I saw you in the flames!"

I felt my eyes widen, not in surprise at the acknowledgment but at the commonality of the experience. Suddenly, his suffering was something I could relate to. The cage got so hot that it felt like someone dowsed the tight space with natural gas and lit a match. Beads of sweat formed on my crown, then quickly slithered down my face. Mr. Charles threw his palm against the glass wall so hard that it caused a crack to grow up to the ceiling from the tiny holes in the center. He broke down, sobbing against the window wall.

An enormous collective gasp came from the galley. The Photographers sprung into action, snapping pictures and taking notes, moving forward to better understand Mr. Charles' breakdown.

Two officers rambled into the glass box to drag Mr. Charles out of the courtroom. He was kicking and screaming, "It's killing us!" as they pulled him out. The door slammed behind them.

The judge slammed her gavel to regain order in her courtroom. The reporters stepped back in place. Mr. Hamilton was making his way to the defense table.

"All right, everyone. Settle down!" She slammed the gavel again. "Order!" The court was quiet immediately. The judge went on. My shirt was wetter from sweat than poor Mr. Charles'. I feared a similar fate. The judge said, "I allowed the press in my courtroom because of public concern for the next case. But you all had better keep it together, or I'll have this courtroom emptied exponentially."

I was the only accused left in the glass box. Why is the press here? What happened to Jamie? Why is he not here? Sudden panic at the thought of the charges I would face flooded my thoughts. Without knowing what happened to Jamie, I did not even guess what they would be.

Hoping to find Jamie, I scoured the courtroom with my eyes. Maybe he'd been beaten a little, bruised up—but alive. I couldn't find him.

From the corner of my eye, I found a figure sitting in the empty jury box. He was faint at first, like a shadow. I almost didn't notice him staring directly at me across the room. His arms were spread open, leaning on the back of the chairs, his feet resting on the back of the seat in front of him. That snide grin plastered across his face. Nail's grimace was like the bitter gaze of justice ready to rule on my fate without hearing the facts first.

My body went numb as I stared back at him. I felt tremendous fear at his ominous presence, dominating the room like an overseer. I knew only I could see him there. Then, fire erupted around his body like a torch in a dark cave. He sat there, smug, dissatisfied, and unbothered by the dancing flames all over him.

A light soprano gasp let loose from the gallery, dowsing Nail's presence like a wind to a match. I looked at the noise and found Sara's blue eyes spread wide and staring at the jury box. Then she looked at me. The questions rose all over her face. Questions I couldn't answer. She had seen him, too. Were we both going mad?

The judge's gavel crashed down once again three times — harder this time. "Miss, do you need to be excused?" The judge asked Sara.

"Yes," Sara said. "I'm sorry, your honor. I should excuse myself." She got up from the bench to walk to the back of the courtroom and quickly out the door. Cameramen snapped photos of her exit. Two men followed behind her. I wanted Faye to get up and go find her. I wanted to go find her myself. Instead, I stood up and took my place near the tiny holes where Mr. Charles had created a crack. I waited there to be addressed.

The bailiff had announced my case during Nail's distraction. There was soft murmuring from the crowd. The judge rolled her eyes at them and pushed her gavel to its station next to the base. Photographers leaned in to take pictures without disturbing the court. The flashes went off in my face like strobe lights, causing me to squint a little away from them. In the flashing, I saw Nail standing in the crowd of picture-takers. Then he disappeared again.

A cloaked, haunting laughter spun quietly behind me in the tiny hot glass box. I almost turned around but realized I didn't need to. I knew who it came from. He was taunting me. Trying to make me look like I'd lost my mind. I kept my eyes forward, waiting for instructions from the judge.

"Your honor, the defense requests remand because of Mr. Grime's out-of-state residency and occupational status. It proposes a flight risk." Prosecutor Thorn requested. In my absent mind, they had already entered an accusation and plea. I didn't hear any of it.

What am I being charged with? What happened to Jamie?

"Your honor, Prosecutor Thorn's ask is unreasonable. My client has an obligation to the Denver Opera House that he would desperately like to fulfill. He has no intention of breaking his contract with the company and will assure appearance at trial when set. Holding him here would only break that contractual agreement and ruin his engagement with the company."

"Your client should have thought about his contractual obligation before he committed a crime in my city, Mr.–"

"Hamilton, Judge Rainer. My client's management flew in from New York to stand by–"

"Oh! Well, it's nice to make your acquaintance, Attorney Hamilton." She said as if dismissing an unwelcomed party guest. The points Hamilton gained with the Denver officers didn't leak into the courthouse, where it could do some good. Judge Rainer turned back to prosecutor Thorn for the answer to her next question. "What's the condition of the victim in this case? I'm reading here that a city citizen was carted off to the hospital because of Mr. Grime's violent actions." She looked at me with a menacing glare that nearly melted me like ice cream on a hot sidewalk. "Is that how they handle things in New York, Mr. Grimes?" Her question didn't sound like it warranted a reply. I kept my mouth shut and lowered my head to avoid her gaze.

"For that reason, the state is requesting remand, your honor. The victim's condition is still unknown at this time." Prosecutor Thorn added. He lowered his eyes to the paperwork at the podium. He looked at a loss for words.

"Does anyone but me give a care about the state of the victim in this case?" I wanted to tell her I did. I stayed silent. "Are we so hellbent on a penalty that we've forgotten about the person beaten and sent to the hospital by our important visitor from the great state of New York?" She paused when no one had an answer to give. I sensed that Judge Rainer was milking her moment in the spotlight and wasn't so concerned with the 'victim'—as she called Jamie.

"The authorities have an ongoing investigation into the incident, your honor. There is an eyewitness to the crime who is more than willing to testify to the defendant's threat on the victim." Prosecutor Thorn sounded as if he was on his last breath when he pushed out his plea to the judge. He was red in the face, with frustration building in his eyes. I didn't understand his anger when he was bound to win. The police report alone would keep me here until trial. I wanted to plead for my life, but I knew—from watching court shows on the web between rehearsal or re-runs of marathons of Law and Order during long stints when work for a classical singer was scarce—that speaking out of turn was unfavorable in front of a judge. I held my tongue. No matter how hot it became in the courtroom, I couldn't afford another mistake.

"Bail is set at fifty thousand dollars."

"The defense is prepared to pay ten thousand right now, your honor," Hamilton added before the judge could clap her gavel. The courtroom went silent for what felt like an eternity.

"And the order is fifty thousand, defense attorney Hamilton." The judge said as she lowered her gavel to lock eyes with my attorney. There was a mocking pity in her emerald eyes. "Was your client under the impression that his professional status and big city representation would somehow get him a pardon, a slap on the wrist because his big show has come to town?"

"Defense claims no such notion, your honor—"

"No. The defense would know better than to claim such a thing in my courtroom, no matter what big city he flew in from. Your client is before the court today because he brought his madness to my city and assaulted one of my citizens. If you or he thinks his actions deserve a forty-thousand-dollar discount because he's the star of the show, both of you are sadly mistaken." She paused, waiting for an answer no one would dare give. "Your client is lucky I haven't seriously considered the prosecutor's remand request, attorney Hamilton."

"The offer is still on the table, judge," Thorne announced, slightly rising from his seat.

"I've made my decision, prosecutor Thorne. Save your enthusiasm for trial." The judge sharply turned to glare at me through the glass of the tiny hot box and said, "Though I am a classical music enthusiast myself, the law is the law. I wish you all the best, Mr. Grime. God be with you." She swiftly struck the sound block with the mallet. The noise caused a rippling echo through the court, causing time to slow down. As she left the bench, the burning figure of Nail appeared at the helm, fire gloriously dancing around his frame in slow sways like red ocean waves. He turned to me, staring at me like the room had become a colossal ice box. I could see his flesh inside, the flames slowly burning away from the muscles in his face, chest, and arms. I nearly screamed. A maddening grin spread across his decaying face beneath his sharp nose.

There was a frenzy across the courtroom among the spectators. The photographers scrambled the gallery to get last-minute mug shots of me. Reporters raced to the exit in the back of the courtroom, jotting notes on their cell phones—some on paper pads. All of them rushed around needlessly. By the close of business the next day, my career in classical music was done. I was sure of it. They'd label me a laughingstock. The biggest disgrace in both the black community and the world of music. They would uncover the horrors that made me and all the dirty secrets I'd been trying to hide for years. A hammer strikes the nail in each article, sealing my fate shut.

The faces in the courtroom were hot with annoyance. Their movements were jagged and forced, like they were angry with one another for no apparent reason, thick with the sickness of rage that had now found its way out of my cell.

Before the officers came to take me, I saw Nail drifting through the room. His body was encased in skipping flames, eating at the rage in the space and feeding the anger everyone was feeling as they parted from the courtroom. Erratic movements and hostility coat their small tasks, pushing open the doors to escape the tension. Even the scribblers wrote with an intense rage at hand. It all rippled from the heat of Nail's phantom burning body. Only I could see what he was doing. He turned to me, grinning manically. The fire stripped him of all covers, clothing, skin, and even some flesh in parts.

I saw Faye with her chubby finger in a reporter's face, reprimanding him, tugging viciously at his camera lance around his neck. I thought for a moment she was choking him. Spittle spat from her mouth while she screamed in his face. He pulled and screamed back.

Sara had returned to the courtroom. Hamilton found her at the back of the court, trying to console her as she wept uncontrollably. The ten grand Hamilton was ready to post for bail was most likely the money she and I set aside for Mya's future. I knew the company wouldn't put a dime toward my rescue. The bail was the cost of the show's budget. If not more.

When the door to the glass chamber opened and the guards came for me, Nail disappeared into his fantasy flames. The dark haze that clouded the courtroom disbursed as if it had never been there. The audience calmed to a trickle from a heavy stream. Sara and Hamilton were the only ones left in the back of the gallery by the double doors. They didn't look at me as the guards took me out and cuffed me to the bench in the hall again.

I hoped I'd have a last-minute meeting with my attorney, but that didn't happen. I sat on the bench shackled at the wrists and ankles for a while. My escorting officer was at the end of the hall by the courtroom doors, talking to a beautiful brunette reporter. The woman casually pointed in my direction, using the end of her pen before tossing her silky mane out of her face. She was flirtatious with the officer until she realized he knew less than she did about my situation. Then she blew him off, walking down the hall from the courtroom. When he turned to me, he looked deflated but distinctly familiar. He was the officer who hopped into the ambulance with Jamie that night.

I tried to leap to my feet from the bench but was yanked down again by my restraints. Overexcited by the realization. He had to know something.

"Whoa, slow it down, choir boy." He said, walking to me, amused again. "Don't tell me you're hurrying to get back to your cell."

"You were one of my arresting officers. I remember you."

He was more handsome in the fluorescent lights of the hallway. Blond hair and blue eyes with a straight white smile filled with irony. He stooped down to unlock my hands from the shackles around my ankles. Then, from the bench. "Stand up." He commanded. I quickly got to my feet, hoping my obedience would garner some answers. "You're a trendy man." He said. He pushed me forward, away from the courtroom and what I believed was the entrance to the building, back to the holding cells. He walked behind me. I felt more uneasy than I thought I should. Something slightly rasped in his voice, different from the night of the arrest. But I was sure it was him.

"I wouldn't say that," I told him. "Right now, I'm a washed-up addict needing answers I think you can help me with. Do you remember me? From the night of my arrest?"

"Keep walking." He demanded when I slowed down a bit. I couldn't remember my way back, but I moved forward anyway. "You enjoyin' your stay here with us, choir boy?" Those hissed words sent a chill up my spine. I tried to look back. "Face forward, boy! Keep it moving forward." He nudged my shoulder, and I stumbled ahead. "You let ole Nail have his way with you, and you'll make it out of here in one piece."

"You know him?"

"I am him, boy. And so are you. Nail's got a hold on us all. Give him a little strike, and you'll wake him up inside. Set your soul ablaze, boy. Do what he says; he'll keep you high as a kite. And if you don't... well, let's say all hell gets loose."

"What is he?"

"Sex. Rape. Fear. Passion ... whatever you need him to be."

"Gone," I said quietly.

We arrived at the end of the corridor, and I remember this was the hallway where we first met. Nail and I. Where he touched me on my way to the cells that first night.

"Wait!" The authoritative, solid voice of the officer had returned. He moved to the keypad and punched in a code to open the steel door in front of us.

"What happened to him?" I asked.

"To who?" He asked, irritated.

"Nail. What happened to Nail—here in the jailhouse?" I felt a sudden panic. The officer investigated me as if I were a madman he didn't recognize as the prisoner he'd transported from the courtroom. It was clear he did not know what I was talking about.

"Who the hell are you talking about? What kind of name is Nail?" He asked. "Don't let this place make you lose your head. It looks like you're coming down off something. Your sweating like it's a hundred and rising."

The funny thing was that I felt chilled to the bone inside. The arraignment wrenched up my taste for a drink or some drug. I feared what the night ahead held for me. For the last two nights, I had roomed with a haunt that was after my soul, and if I didn't fight for my life that night, he would be victorious.

"This ain't even the bottom of the shithole. You're still dangling around the rim, Sweet Cheeks." He laughed maniacally, half turning to open the door. Then he turned back to me and said, "I remember your friend from the night of your fight. My partner, Downs, recognized you right away. I don't care too much about that classical music shit. Violins give me a headache. I'm more of a hip-hop type of guy myself. Your friend looked pretty banged up when we loaded him into the bus. I don't know how he survived that beating you put on him."

"Then, he's alright?" I lit up inside.

"We got to the hospital, and your buddy woke up frantic. He realized where we'd taken him while we pulled the gurney off the bus. He got furious with the EMTs. Cursed them out and jumped off the gurney and out of the ambulance, walking off. He didn't even wait for your other friend."

"He's not my friend."

"Whatever he was. Your guy refused treatment. He snatched some gauze and ointment off a shelf in the bus and took off into the night."

"You didn't go after him?"

"Figured if he died on his way home, someone would call it in. Can't force him to take the help. You two are a couple, right?"

I hesitated. The officer noticed. He stepped behind me to unlock the cuffs on my ankles. I wanted to run, but where would I go?

"I don't judge. Everybody's got their own cross." He said. "Seems like he'd be here today if he cared anything about you. Hope it was worth all the trouble."

I didn't bother to respond. He laced his comment with sarcasm, but it was all too true. Why hadn't Jamie come to the arraignment? Where was he now? He probably stomped off that ambulance with Steven and returned to the crime scene and laughed the night away, smoking up and having sex. The thought of it made me nauseous. I put my life in the hands of a cheating bastard who never cared for my well-being at all. The punishment served me right.

"I'll make it better, boy." I heard the hissing voice once again as the door opened to the main room of the holding cell. "Surrender to me..."

"Step inside, inmate." The officer said. "You know where you go."

My tomb door was wide open, and the darkness of the tiny room was waiting for me. I feared what waited for me in that darkness. I had no choice but to face it. Whatever it was. I stepped into my cell, and the door slammed shut behind me.

FIGHT FOR MY SOUL

Ж

Thick masses of gray clouds hovered in the sky outside the thin window as I looked into the world I was denied access to at my arraignment. A storm would take the night in Denver. The wet would saturate the massive lawn's fluffy trees and green grass outside the Capital building. I thought about how good being out in that storm would feel. To feel the wind push the water into my face. I wouldn't even turn away to protect my eyes. I'd let it rain over me like a river come to wash me of the sins I'd committed against my family, admirers, myself, and even my haters.

A flare of lightning quickly shot across the darkening sky, followed by a rumbling thunder crack that slightly shook the earth. The jailhouse seemed to stomp up and down like a giant, angry child. Not long after, the rain started a trickle.

The alarm sounded, and the cell doors flushed open, signaling the time for our last meal of the day before lights out. The monotonous routine of this life had already settled into my system. For a second, I was thankful for my former cellmate's companionship. Though tainted, it was a type of escape. I quickly grew frightened at the cost of playing with his deviled magic. What would he want from me in return? I felt utterly alone for the first time since my stay at the Denver County Jailhouse. There was no one else. I was tempted to skip the meal to savor the feeling and do my best to guard the space away from my evil cellmate. But I knew he would be back. I had to confront him once more. I was ready.

I'd keep a level head and not fly off the handle at the meal table to avoid another riot. The guards probably had me on suicide watch after what was said at the meeting before my arraignment: rape and ghosts. The courts may even order a psych evaluation now.

My battle with Nail had to be fought in the privacy of our cell. Reluctantly, I left the window to exit the cell into the mess hall. The white walls made me feel like a drop of rain. A tear in the eye of madness waiting for that blink that would set me free. I joined the other sad droplets at our table of despair, dressed in styrofoam containers of brown slop and sour brown milk from a lazy cow. This tedious ritual of life would drive any man to suicide. Hoping for answers that would never come.

I dipped my spoon into the brown of the bowl to begin my shoveling and looked up to find the old man who looked like my father, aged, sitting across from me. He shoved a few spoonsful of the muddy substance into his mouth and chewed large.

"Are you real?" I had to ask. He was so animated in his chewing that I thought I had slipped into another dream.

"Speak soft and shove food in your mouth so they don't suspect we're talking." He told me while ramming more stew into his mouth. The words came through bits of meat falling into his scrappy salt-and-pepper beard. He didn't look so deranged up close. He looked more like an actor in a role that required his best insanity performance. His clothes looked purposely disheveled but not filthy. There was no odor emitting from him. Those soft brown eyes - like my dad's, like mine - settled on me as if aiming to bring calm over my soul. I continued to stuff my face. I didn't even taste the meal after a while.

"He has known you now."

"Nail?" I asked. "You saw him that day. At my cell door —"

"Is that what he calls himself now? I know the devil by only one name. Fight him off you."

"How?"

"Use his tricks against him."

"How do I do that?" My voice slightly raised through the stew. "Stop with the riddles and tell it to me straight. I know you can." I looked around the table at the other men, preoccupied with their meals. Some of them struck up their own dinner conversations with one another. The guards in the booth weren't even watching anymore, preoccupied with a box of cheesy pizza for their dinner hour. Occasionally, they glanced at us to be sure everything stayed in order. I looked down at my bowl and wanted to vomit.

"Shovel and talk, black man." The old black man told me, jabbing at me with a boney black finger. "You need to get him off your back before he takes you back down to that hell he's living through. That's how he gets out. That's how he wonders around in the free world."

"Tell me the trick. How'd you shake him?"

"You're looking at it." The old man said with a grin. "I made him think I'd lost my mind enough to kill myself. Good thing the guards thought the same and snatched me from your cell. They shackled me at this table the first night I spent in that cell with it. Before the night was over, they brought a white boy in here and put him in there. By noon the next morning, the cell next to yours came empty. So, they put me in there. Two days passed. I only saw that boy come out of that cell once for a meal. He was ghost white then and looked like death walking."

"What happened to him?"

"They found him dead in the cell the next day. They had no idea what for."

"But you know, don't you?" I said. "You saw him. You saw that thing living in the walls–"

"This whole place is a portal to hell. It feeds on a criminal's fears and turns you into one even if you came in here an innocent man. Nail—or whatever you want to call it — is the devil's herald. He seeks you out and temps you through your weakness. Once he knows you, he turns you to it—that thing in the walls."

"How many men has this happened to?"

"He keeps his numbers low to stave off the guards." He said. "One or two every so often turn up dead in their cells since I was here. On different blocks. No pattern."

"And how long has that been?"

"What that got to do with anything?" He said after a pause. "I'm here long enough to see and warn you of what you're up against. You can't let him take you. No matter how strong your desire is. No matter how he turns you on with his tricks."

The old man got up from the table with his empty bowl. Most of his meal had made a home in his beard; his eyes had gone vacant and wild again.

"Where are you going?" I pleaded. "I have more questions."

"You know the drill, inmate." He said in a calm voice. "Don't make another scene."

He tossed his bowl in the trash and returned to his cell immediately. I glanced at the guard station. One guard stared back at me. His square jaw was tight as his eyes narrowed their gaze on me. I saw Nail's heat rising in those green eyes.

I got up from the table then. I threw away my empty bowl to retreat into my haunted hole quickly. Before the door was closed, I heard snickering and harsh remarks from the inmates still at the table. They call me 'the faggot' and 'sissy.' I hadn't heard those insults since I was a boy. One deep voice said the words loud enough to hear them while I sat on my iron cot. I wanted to leave my cell and confront them, but what was there to contradict? The man was laying the cards on the table. Why should I fight the truth? What was the shame in living my truth?

I got up from the cot to return to my view from the skinny window. The rain tumbled down onto the city streets. A washing had begun.

The entire holding cell went quiet immediately after dinner. The trickling sound of the rain outside was my only company as I drifted off into deep, troubling sleep. Finally, feeling alone ushered in a welcomed rest. The temperature dropped outside, causing a chill in the cell. My thin clothes were hardly enough to keep me warm. I lay on my back and quivered in waking sleep that felt more like the aching pain of the flu. With the quivering in my body rocking me to sleep one minute, a sudden hard shake would pull me out again.

The thundering rainstorm changed to a heavy hail and snow blizzard that beat against the jail like angry little feet. I exited the cot to see the storm through the skinny window. The city park below was snowcapped, and the flakes falling looked the size of fall leaves in white, blowing in clusters through the wind.

It had been years since I prayed. Though I sang in churches nationwide, sermons never moved me to any strong belief or faith—for that matter. I know there is a God. Mother made me understand that growing up, though she behaved like He wasn't watching. And somehow, I'd resolved that karma had finally caught up with her that night, so many years ago, in that Denver hotel room where my daddy took her life. Took the life of my wife's father. I wondered if he had discovered what they were doing behind his back that night. Did the exposure of the affair spawn his rage?

I prayed in my cell. It was the best time for it if there ever was one. I asked for forgiveness. I pleaded for faith. I asked God not to give up on me because I was so close to giving up on myself. And what I heard in my subconscious, these words: 'Hold your faith' whispered back at me in my mother's voice. Through all the drug use, the drinking, the erroneous sexual encounters, and the lies I told to keep my true identity hidden, I found hope genuflect on the cold floor before that skinny window and the raging storm outside.

I felt the weight of the evil head of the beast linger in the space above my head—Bone-chilling, more vigorous, and sudden. Before I could turn to face it, the burning breath of it swam over my shoulder. So hot that it singed my neck.

An unbearable heat rose from the core of me into my chest, then scorched my mind as the heat burst into my skull. I fell back at the hip like a broken doll. The same way I found Nail that first night when I saw the beast. Nail had turned me over to whatever evil it was that powered him. I was so afraid of what I might find if I opened my eyes that I slammed them shut and continued to pray in a quiet murmur. I could hear growling like a million angry dogs coming for me. There were moments when they'd bark in my ear, nearly causing me to look for them. I kept my lids sealed tight. I couldn't move from that position the entire night. At some point, I fell into a deep sleep. The dreams I had that night were saturated with rage and highly violent. The storm outside my window brought peace somehow. Listening to it beat down on the jail felt like nature fighting my battles for me while I protected myself from whatever the next round would bring.

Morning came, and I found myself sprawled out on the floor on my back. I'd survived the torture to see another day. The blizzard had calmed, but the snow still fell in monstrous flakes. I thought about the opera house canceling the night preview because of inclement weather. But why would they do that? It was Colorado. Heavy snow was as natural as flowers in spring there. The show would go on.

The evil presence had left me sometime before the sun came up. I stood and walked to the window half-caked with a thick white powder from the storm. I had to rise up on my tiptoes to glimpse the snow-capped world around me. I was awake with the sun before the breakfast alarm sounded. I felt groggy but better than the day before. Stronger somehow.

It was the first night of previews for Otello. I don't remember eating a single meal or leaving my cell that day. My mind was stuck on the outside world as I wondered what prevented my bail. I found my way back to the slithered window, searching for someone coming to rescue me from this torture.

Where was Jamie? He'd been out of the hospital since this torment began, and not a word. This was no time to hold a grudge. He held the fate of my career at his mercy, and his ego was making all the decisions. Or maybe he was dead.

The hours sailed by with not a note from the outside world—or the supernatural one. The snow continued to fall, eventually clouding the slice of the window with enough snow that I could no longer see out.

Before long, the diner alarm sounded, the door slammed open, and I lost all hope of making it to the theatre in time for a curtain call. I couldn't eat another bowl of muddy slop another night.

Opening night.

I imagined everyone in the green room humming the bars of the choruses and warming up their voices before the show began. I never wanted to be somewhere so badly in all my life. The damage I'd done was made visceral at that moment. I abused drugs all that time, and my voice never faltered. God had been watching over me, and I had shunned His gift by smoking away my dreams.

Overwrought with guilt, I got up from the table to throw out my slop bowl. There were fewer inmates at the table that night. The old man was not there. Was he released? The shame followed as I retreated to my cell and plopped down on my bunk. The door slammed shut.

I cried at the curtain call time. I knew the show was about to begin without me. In my mind, I could hear the orchestra tuning up as the audience took their seats. The house might not be whole, but there were enough people there to entertain with the extraordinary tale by Verdi we had prepared. Performed once more with another black-faced singer mocking the leading role. The shame I felt crushed me. I couldn't stop the tears. I had lost the most excellent lover of my life with a slit-second choice of violence.

"Awe... just look at you. Did your date spill his seed all over your prom dress, Sweet Cheeks? That's what you git for messin' with them dirty white boys." The voice came through a grin from the bunk across from mine. Nail had returned. I was so angry that I didn't even feel him arrive.

"I wondered when you'd come back," I said without looking at him. I just couldn't at the moment. There was still strength building in me.

"I'll always be here, boy. Even when you think I'm not, you can bet your fine ass I'm gone be there waiting to get inside and blaze you right up. You people are like a book of matches. Anything will set you in a blaze. The law ought to lock all you darkies up in these prisons and let you kill yourselves off. Your black ass don't belong in no white man's world."

"Is that what you think?" I looked up from my tears and could see Nail full-on in front of me, sitting at the edge of the bed. It was like I could see him all along in this form, but I didn't want to believe it to be true. His appearance was so authentic that he was as transparent as thought and imagination. He was there and not. Full and faded all at once.

"I know that for a fact, boy." Fire-red hair on his head and face seemed to have a life of their own in the glow of his translucent and luminescent face. I felt more pity for him than fear before knowing what he was—trapped here even after death. A prisoner of a darker warden than the one I was under. I realized then what Nail was after.

"That white boy's gonna press charges against you for beatin' him in the street."

"Why hasn't he done it already?"

"You think he loves you? You Fags are all the same. Desperate and blind as bats. Especially you black boys. Always looking for the white man's approval but claiming you don't care what we think of you."

"You sound ignorant," I said. Beads of sweat start to form on my crown.

"That's right, boy." Nail hissed. "Get that rage up and surrender yourself to your master, Sweet Cheeks. His power is all the love you'll ever get."

From the dark corner by the slim window manifested the large lizard-like face of the demon penetrating the well of black space. Its oversized bull horns on either side of its head coiled out of the space first. The eyes of the creature were so deep set in the reptile's face they seemed not to exist. The temperature in the room dropped to nearly freezing as my anger streamed to fear. It clutches at me from inside, drawing me closer to its savory mouth, drooling large, wet saliva from a fat black tongue. The stench of it snatched my breath away. Suddenly, I was on the cell floor between the two beds. The demon and Nail stood over me like titans to a grizzly bear. I could not believe what I was seeing.

"Heathen. Heaven has no place for nigger faggots!" Nail said.

"God hates the sin, but not the sinner." I cried back. I don't know where it came from in my memory, but the words slightly released the demon's hold on my soul. I curled to my knees; lifted my head to face the evil. Eye to eye.

"Your God created Adam and Eve. Not Adam and –"

"I'd rather live my truth than tell more lies to my soul," I shout back at him. The demon's hold on me let up some more.

"There is no fear in love, but perfect love casteth out fear: because fear hath torment. He that feareth is not made perfect in love. 1 John 4:18."

The scripture offended the demon as its grip on my soul coward again.

The jail outside my cage came alive in the night. I could hear the guards summoning me to quiet down. I wouldn't! Another force—a light source had opened a chamber inside me as my voice rose out of my body, and I sang the opening notes of Otello's aria into the opera's opening scene. Iago has coaxed Cassio to speak ill of Otello, beginning his spin of lies that eventually cause the tragic hero to go mad and kill his wife.

What lay dormant for days in me finally released a whale of sound that shook the walls of my cell. The demon backed into its dark corner until I couldn't feel his presence inside me any longer. The wind outside whistled like orchestration beneath my song. I envisioned myself on the stage with the cast in the colossal street scene. I could see their faces as if they had transported me to the theatre, center stage. They smiled triumphantly at my performance, giving my voice the strength it craved to sing out strong.

My tenor billowed and boomed through the cell walls, penetrating the surrounding cement until it didn't exist to me anymore. There was nothing but the stage. Then the cast disbursed, and Sara–my Desdemona–entered the scene to duet my aria. We sang of our forbidden love and the longing. One day to celebrate that love in the light. I could actually feel her with me then. I heard her voice as clearly as I'd heard my own. It was like we had broken all the barriers that kept us apart.

I opened my eyes as we sang the final cords together, and her voice faded from my ears as the vision fizzled into mist and brought me back to my holding cell. A thunderous clamor of sound exploded outside the dorm. The inmates cheered me on. Banging on the cots and doors of their cells.

My body flopped down to the cold floor from sheer exhaustion. My breathing was erratic but slowed to a calming pace when I felt that sense of being alone again. There was no other presence in the tiny cell but mine. It felt like a regular closeted box holding any criminal. Only I felt released.

The brutal winds blew the sticking flakes from the window, and I could see the snow had stopped falling. There was a clear, starry night showing through the glass. The moonlight had found its way into the room to caress me with its soft gray light. I slept peacefully for the first time since I set foot in the state of Colorado.

DAWN

Ж

At daybreak, the sunbeam shining through the thin window covered me like a warm blanket as I lay still on my cell's cold, hard floor. I came through sleep feeling more rested than I had in years. I felt newborn in my new life. I let the sun's rays kiss my body as I turned over onto my back and took a long, deep breath of my new day. The air filled my lungs with a renewed desire to keep up the fight for more days like that morning.

"I'm free," I said softly to the cell walls. They seemed to sigh back a similar relief.

When the steel door opened with a loud draw into the wall, I thought it was too early for our morning meal. I tilt my head back to look at the open doorway better. A large, shadowed body stood between the glare of the main room and my prison. His figure created a shadow so large that it nearly covered me. Blocking the sunbeam that comforted me from the outside world. I was looking up at this man from a freshly unearthed grave. He found a man reborn unto himself, climbing out of the dirt of his past. I almost laughed at my rescuer, finding me in such a vulnerable state. I held back that smile, not wanting to offend him. I knew it was one of the guards probably coming to reprimand me for all the noise from the night before.

"The bunks are not good enough for you, Mr. Grime?"

There was an optimistic effect on the guard's inquiry. He sounded familiar to me. I sat up and turned away from the window to the gaping door, and the guard stepped inside, where I could see him better.

It was Officer Downs. I wondered why they sent him to scold me. I thought he was a field officer. Sitting up crossed-legged on the floor, I investigated Down's face closer. There was a tenderness I hadn't seen in his eyes since we met in his cop car when I looked into those eyes through the rearview mirror, pitifully glaring back at me. They were like a father's eyes looking down at his broken boy, wondering how he could help. My cheeks got hot with excitement and a shade of embarrassment as a smile breach my face.

"They sent you here to scold me for the noise last night?" I asked. "I apologize. It–"

"What the devil are you talking about, Mr. Grime? Last night was one of the quietest nights this hellhole has seen in months."

"Quiet? I don't understand. The inmates went crazy after I'd finished my aria and passed out on the floor. Maybe you weren't here–"

"I was on watch the whole night. I didn't hear a peep out of any of yous. And if you were singing up a storm in here, I'd have called my wife and held the phone up so she could hear, completely blowing my cover. The surprise

would have been worth it, though. I told you she's a big fan–
"

"You did," I said. "I remember that."

"So, no. I didn't hear anything from the cells last night."

I got up from the floor to sit on the iron cot. Renewed feelings quickly replaced the confusion and despair.

Had it all been a dream?

Observing the room for more signs of change, I saw that the cot across from mine was gone or was never there. The tiny room was smaller than it had been, and there was no sign it had ever been a two-man cell.

Officer Downs came further into the cell until he was at my side. I noticed something in his hand—an album cover. I didn't look at it long enough at first to see the artist. I wondered why he brought it and if he wanted me to listen. Where would we even play it? He gestured to me a request to sit beside me on the cot. I obliged his gesture with a welcoming one. I scooted over to make room. I didn't want to be too far away from him. His presence made me feel in safer hands than my own. As he sat down, he revealed the album jacket in his hand. It was the jacket of Dad's music project with Mom and Sara's dad, Jackson Grime. I didn't remember until I saw the jacket picture; our parents had decided to use a picture of us, Sara, my other brother Russel and me at a family gathering as the cover image. They told us it represents the music of the album best. The photo was just the three of us as young teens under a large, wild tree full of green leaves. The branches were long enough to sit on and winding enough to tempt a child to play. The three of us at the base of the grand trunk posing in semi-sneers and adolescent awkwardness, looking full on into the camera lens as directed by my father, snapping the classic shot. The back jacket was the same picture, only a close-up shot where our expressions were more evident.

The tears welled, remembering when the picture was taken and how glorious that day in the park had been with my blended family. We were all together then. Happier than we'd ever been in this life.

The album's title, Songbirds, was in the top right corner in a scripted font, with the trio's name in the bottom left corner in the same script. I couldn't figure out why Downs had brought it here, of all places. It was an exceedingly popular album back then. So, it didn't surprise me he had a copy. I hadn't seen a copy since my brother's funeral, after his suicide, only a year after our parents' deaths. It was one of my favorite LPs back then. I'd banned it from my memory once the creators were gone.

Then Downs said, "I told you I knew who you were. That's you. Right?" He said, pointing at my younger self to the left of Sara, in my favorite green sweater and button-down light green shirt. I was scratching the back of my head and looking curiously at the world and what was ahead of me. "And that looks like your wife as a little girl."

"It is," I said, staring at the memory.

"And that gentleman is your older brother?"

"Yes," I confirmed.

"Yeah. He looked just like your mother." He said, letting me know he knew of his tragic end. But how?

"See, I'm a jazz man myself—"

"Such is the case with music couples," I said with a grin. "One is into classical, and the other loves Jazz even more."

We both chuckled.

"Right!" Downs went on. "Seeing your wife in person yesterday got me wondering where I'd seen your faces before then. I thought about a case that came here when I was just a rookie. A musician by the name of Roger Master was brought in for a murder that took place in a hotel in downtown Denver. He'd confessed to killing his wife and her lover. The two co-stars made up the jazz trio. They were supposed to perform at some small venue that shut a few months after the murders."

"That man was my father," I said.

"I know." He said. "When they hauled him in here, he was hot in the pit of hell. Kinda like you when I pulled you in." I looked into his face and realized his age and how he would have looked back then. He was maybe ten years my father's junior and would have been a young cop when my mother's life was taken. "The jailhouse was set up differently before the upgrades. There were still bars separating the cells. The guards could keep a good eye on the prisoners. That first night, your dad raged about his cell being haunted by demons that talked to him in the night. Of course, we thought he'd finally lost his head on account of what he'd done to your mother and his music partner. He got to hollering, so I had to take him out of the cell the next night and chain him to the table. Just to shut him up."

The old man.

"The next day, he seemed to have calmed down and let the morning duty guards put him in the cell next to the one he complained about. It was hushed that next night, too—now that I think about it. No one saw or heard anything suspicious until the next day when they found him dangling from the ceiling by his pant leg tied around his neck and anchored to the ceiling. The seat of his pants embedded to a hook in the roof of his cell."

"No. That's not what he said happened. He survived his torture." I cried.

"Your father's been dead for years now." Downs said. "There's no way he could have told you anything."

"No. It wasn't him. This man was older than my father."

"Pardon my saying, but we haven't had too many old black men in this jail recently. You young people like to stir up all the trouble these days."

"I'm sure you're right." I resolved not to defend my delusions. "Go on. Was there more?"

"After your dad's suicide, a few other new inmates complained when we put them in that cell. Complained they were hearing voices and having visions and a demon in the walls. All crazy things," he paused, then said, "The way you talked yesterday in the meeting room." I ignored his last statement.

"What about Nail?" I asked. "Where did he come from?"

"Nail? Who the hell told you about him?"

"That doesn't matter. Do you know about him too?"

Downs hesitated a moment. He glared at me like I'd opened a can of worms he didn't think I should have access to. Suspicion sprouted in his expression. "The more we tell you all not to talk to one another, the more ways you find to do just that." He took a deep breath, then said, "He was here long before my time, but the rumors about him seem to live on like ghosts. He was in the Aryan Brotherhood chapter here in Denver. He was arrested for raping and killing a black boy behind a private Gay club in downtown Denver."

"Rape?"

"He violated a local black boy he tempted into an alley behind the club. The sodomy was brutal. Then he brought the boy's body to Cheesman Park and hung him in a tree on the park's main pathway. The damnedest thing is that he turned himself in here the same night. He hung himself in the–" He stopped suddenly, deep in the memory as if recognizing something he hadn't before.

"Where?" I eagerly asked. "Where did he hang himself?"

"The same cell as your father, come to think about it." We sat quietly on the iron cot for what seemed like minutes. Both of us were lost in the mysterious circumstances of the situation.

Downs suddenly got up from the cot, taking the album jacket from under my still hands. I almost snatched it back from him. "If you don't mind." He said.

"I'm sorry." I handed it to him.

"It's alright. I didn't intend to come in here and bog you down with jailhouse history. Just thought you'd want to know what I knew. I've got good news, too. They bonded you out."

"What?" I felt like I'd won the lottery.

"Somebody came in last night with the money. I went home during my break to get the album sleeve to show you. I was hoping you'd sign it for my lady."

"Of course I will," I said in a daze. "You said I've been bonded out? By who?"

"Now that I don't know." Downs said. "Get yourself together. We'll get a pen, and you can sign this before I escort you out of here. You're free to go."

My wallet and hotel room key were the only personal effects to retrieve from the clerk. They gave me a paper that explained my rights as an accused out on bail. Mostly letting me know that I was not allowed to leave the state until my trial date. The consequence was my bail money revoked and a warrant issued for my arrest; held in contempt in jail until they rendered a trial. Extra charges would be added to my violations as well.

I found Downs near the clerk's office at the end of the hall. He had a marker, the album jacket in hand, and a smile to greet me on my way out. I was stunned at his enthusiasm to assist a complete stranger he'd only known through his admiration for music. I was grateful to his wife—a music teacher—and searched my thoughts for a way to show them my gratitude as Downs escorted me further down the hall as a free man.

We arrived at a door that looked nothing like an entrance. A freight elevator across from double doors looked to lead out to a loading dock. The long white hallway was empty and inactive, uncommonly quiet for such a workspace. I turned to Downs with wonder in my mind.

"I brought you around back because I saw a few reporters lingering on the courthouse steps early this morning. Those men are like vultures with getting a story." Downs said with a smile. I marveled at his kindness. I wanted to give him a big hug. I reached for the album cover instead.

"Here. Let me sign that for you before we part."

"Oh yes. Right." He said, handing me the jacket and pulling a pen from his shirt pocket. I took them and began signing. There was so much I wanted to say, but I could only muster up a few words of thanks for following my career.

"What's your wife's name?"

"Alice. Alice Downs." He said. "You think the company will let you perform now that we nearly straightened this out?"

"I can't be sure."

"My wife will surely be disappointed if they don't. She told me the kids were really excited to see their first opera. She works with minority students who are underprivileged but gifted in the arts. It would break her heart to see a white man in blackface playing the role."

"It breaks my heart too, officer," I said. "When are they expected to come?"

"The closing night performance." Downs said. "They even planned a dinner at the Rialto café downtown."

"Fancy," I said, smiling at him. "I can't promise anything. But I will try not to let your wife and the class down."

"You stay out of trouble, Songbird." He told me as I gave back the jacket and pen. He opened one of the double doors leading outside. That crisp, cool air felt like heaven blowing into my face.

"Later, Downs," I said.

"I mean no offense, but I hope never to make your acquaintance this way again, Cameron Grime."

"You got it, old man."

We smiled at one another before I walked out the back door, a free man again. When the sun struck me full-on in the face, I embraced its glorious light with a smile to the sky. The docking area was also empty and so quiet that I could hear the snow melting off the trees. Some patches fall in clumps, making a spattering sound as they hit the ground. The morning was warm and fresh like spring, though fall was settling into the Mile-High city. I felt no demons on my back, and the taste for drugs was something I was ready to battle against to save my life. I walked on.

Pride wouldn't let me resist the urge to sneak around to the front of the courthouse to see the mob of reports that Downs said had gathered there. It was a disappointing sight at best. A handful of men stood around the courthouse entrance at the top of the steps. Dressed in suits and smoking cigarettes with those notepads dangling from their hands. The whole scene looked like a movie set of a crime drama where the criminal's story was just a blip on the news radar.

The reporters looked board under the awning—the snow around the steps added to the dismal drama of the scene.

One reporter reading a newspaper, leaning against a pillar, looked up from his article directly at me, standing near the bottom of the steps. I thought he spotted me. Before I could turn my face away, he spat over his paper into the snow beneath him, took a drag from his smoke, looked back at his paper, and casually read. I was unnoticed. Or maybe they didn't care anymore about my story. It was old news. I smiled and walked on.

I felt the hotel room key in my pocket and hoped I still had the room. I was looking forward to a warm bath and a moment alone to gather my thoughts before meeting with the company about the show. I knew they could not allow me to perform, but I had to try something. I walked faster through the wet, slushy snow, further away from the courthouse and into the park. I couldn't feel the slight chill in the air. I felt akin to it somehow.

"Cameron." Jamie's sharp voice snatched me out of my thoughts. He emerged from behind a large bush that was still capped with snow. I noticed his white face was bruised and slightly swollen. He wore oversized black shades, but I could still see the swollen eyes behind them. It was a shock to realize how badly I had beaten his face. I'd always loved his soft blue eyes and high cheekbones in his narrow facial structure. What I once found handsome now seemed deceptive and full of manipulation. I wanted to walk right by him without a word, but I knew I couldn't do that. He was one of the demons on the free side of this life I had to confront. He repeated my name, then reached for my arm. I stopped walking before he could touch me.

"I bet you're sorry about what you did to me." He said through a snarled grin. It reminded me of Nail's grin. "I forgive you. I was so doped up that night I didn't even feel your little sissy slaps." He laughed. I didn't.

"Where have you been all this time?" I asked. "Why weren't you at my arraignment?"

"I was there, silly. How do you think I knew what to post to bond you out?"

"You did that?"

"Of course." He proudly expressed. "You didn't think those poor snobs at the opera company would ever come to your rescue, did you? I told you those people don't care about you."

"My agent was there. With a lawyer."

"Yeah. I saw her fat ass with your wife." He said. "She's beautiful. Your wife—"

"You leave her out of this." I stepped closer to him. He took a half step back.

"Calm down, Cam. We don't need to make another scene." He said with a chuckle. He twitched at the slight pain in his face. I felt sorry for him all over again.

"Why didn't you let the doctor look at you?"

"I have no fuckin' insurance, Cameron. Doctors cost money."

"How'd you get money for bail?"

He pursed his lips and shook his head like I was clueless. His expression told me what I asked. He was a drug dealer—lots of Friends in Low Places. "I'm a hustler. It's what I do." He said. He pulled a newspaper from the inside pocket of his jacket and handed it to me. "It's yesterday's news, but your story finally made the front page. I thought you'd want to collect that. It's a classic."

"We're through, James." The words just fell from my mouth. The reward of finally getting them out was instant. "I'm through with this." I didn't take the newspaper.

"You can't do that." He said as I pushed past him. "I'm sorry about Steven. I'll make it up to you. I've got some good shit back at the apartment. You should—"

"I'm good on that."

"Yeah, right." The smirk on his smug face accentuated his broad, arrogant jawline. My fist hadn't ruined that. My beautiful disaster. My train wreck. I wanted to take him in my arms and squeeze the mean streak out of him. I knew it was best to walk away.

Then Jamie's face morphed into a swirl of nose, eyes, mouth, and brow until it sharpened to reveal Nail's stern look. He glared back at me through Jamie's frame with a wicked red in his eyes that burned hot. I jumped back from him and gasped hard. The face quickly changed back.

"What's wrong with you?" Jamie asked. He grabbed my arm hard enough to feel his nails dig into my skin. I yanked my arm away.

"I need to go," I said.

"I'll press charges against you!" He threatened. "They'll lock your black ass up in another cage, boy!" He sounded like Nail, but I still didn't look back. I was far enough away that it sounded like a whisper in the wind.

They eventually dropped the charges the county pressed against me. The arresting officers convinced the district attorney's office there was no real case to pursue. The victim wasn't interested in pressing charges. They were having trouble finding Jamie for questioning.

Previews ran alternate nights for Otello a week before opening. It received rave reviews and played for packed houses throughout the run. They hailed Miles in the local papers as the unsung hero who finally got his big moment in the spotlight. He saved the company as their tar-faced hero on the opera stage. His contract was more significant than they offered me when he took over the role. Faye became his agent when she found out he had no formal representation. She finagled an understudy deal for me during the run. Sara and I call it my 'instant karma' for all the trouble I caused. I was lucky Faye had any faith in me left in her.

Sara told me that during the first preview, she felt that for the first few scenes of the show, Miles wasn't himself playing the role. She heard my voice singing the part, primarily through their first duet. A few chorus members mentioned the same thing to her about Miles. Miles even mentioned during drinks that night after the show that he felt possessed during the opening.

I didn't share with her what I did in my cell that night to save my soul. I didn't speak to her at all about Nail again. I felt somehow she already knew.

The week of closing, I was called in to sing because Miles was struck down with strep throat and ordered bedridden by his doctor. I didn't inform Downs that I'd be performing after all. I was just prepared to have a fantastic week on the stage. And that's what it turned out to be. Sara and I couldn't have pulled off better performances. The production went out with a bang to a packed house, and there in the front row was Downs. Beside him was a lovely dark skin woman with jet-black hair pulled back in a bun. She wore a lovely evening gown complimenting her curvy figure and gleamed at me the entire performance. I assumed the young people around her in the first two rows were her class. Their wide eyes marveled at my rising voice—wholly captivated.

Sara and I have divorced. She filed the papers when the show ended and was back in New York. I told Mya about my leaving the house and told her I'd always be there for her, no matter what the future holds. I hoped she understood me.

I am in a recovery house now. I decided to stay in Colorado to continue the healing. I've fallen in love with the mountains. I'm working on my sobriety. I attend church regularly—a non-denominational church. I sing in the choir for free. It's been quite the struggle, but the demons I grapple with now are weaker than my strength, and my faith continues to grow. Thank God.

ABOUT THE AUTHOR

Ж

Ted Campbell is a native New Yorker from Westchester County. He is a Purchase College graduate with a Master's in Acting from the National Theatre Conservatory in Denver, Colorado. *A Violation* is Ted's first novel. Pending works can be found on his page on Wattpad.com. @alex2010.tc

www.ingramcontent.com/pod-product-compliance
Lightning Source LLC
Chambersburg PA
CBHW060412310726
48976CB00003B/1027